TOY GUNS

WINNER OF THE 1999 WILLA CATHER FICTION PRIZE

The Willa Cather Fiction Prize was established in 1991 by
Helicon Nine Editions, and is awarded annually to a
previously unpublished manuscript chosen by a distinguished
writer through an open nationwide competition.

The judge for 1999 was Al Young.

TOY GUNS

S T O R I E S

LISA NORRIS

Winner of the Willa Cather Fiction Prize
Selected by Al Young

HELICON NINE EDITIONS
KANSAS CITY & LOS ANGELES

Grateful acknowledgment is made to the editors of the following magazines
in which these stories first appeared: *Bluepenny Quarterly*, *CrossConnect III*,
Kansas Quarterly/Arkansas Review, *Oklahoma Review*, *South Dakota Review*,
Treasure House 6, and *Westview: A Journal of Western Oklahoma*.
Acknowledgments continued on page 144.

Cover and book design: Tim Barnhart

Helicon Nine Editions is grateful to the National Endowment for the Arts,
a federal agency, the Missouri Arts Council and the Kansas Arts
Commission, state agencies, and to the N.W. Dible Foundation
and the Miller Mellor Foundation for their support.

LIBRARY OF CONGRESS CATALOGING-IN-PUBLICATION DATA

Norris, Lisa
    Toy guns : stories / Lisa Norris -- 1st ed.
    p. cm.
    "Winner of the 1999 Willa Cather Fiction Prize."
    Contents: Trailer people--American primitive--Toy guns--Wind across
the breaks--Interior country--Prisoner of war--Stray dogs--Self-defense--
Swimmers--Black ice
    ISBN 1-884235-31-X : (paperback : alk. paper)
      1. United States--social life and customs--20th century--Fiction.
      2. Firearms ownership--Fiction. 3. Firearms owners--Fiction. 4. Family
    violence--Fiction I. Title.

PS3564.O67 T69 2000
813'.6--dc21   00-057565

Manufactured in the United States of America
FIRST EDITION
HELICON NINE EDITIONS
KANSAS CITY & LOS ANGELES

For Ed

CONTENTS

INTERIOR COUNTRY

WHEN THEY FIRST WALKED IN, THE EMPTINESS of the place made sense to Cory. After all, it was late September in Alaska. Winter could begin anytime. The lobby was dark, posters tacked to the log walls the only decoration: climbers heading for the summit of Mt. McKinley; a moose's roman-nosed, antlered head in profile; herds of caribou streaming across the tundra taken from high in the air. A high desk occupied one corner, but its surface was clean. No one stood behind it. On either side of the desk, long red-carpeted hallways opened to Cory's left and right. To the right of the desk, another corridor, marked To Hot Spring Pool sported an arrow leading toward a source of light.

Roxanne, the woman who'd picked her up on the road to the hot spring, nodded in the direction of the pool. She wore jeans and a Western shirt trimmed with embroidery. Her bleached hair was done like a country-western singer's, with curly bangs and long wavy strands to her shoulders. She was older than Cory, old enough that her make-up didn't quite mask the pouches under her eyes or the loose skin on her neck. One hand rested on a canvas bag that hung from her shoulder. She said, "Let's just see who's around."

The smell of chlorine grew stronger as they approached the pool. Through the glass doors Cory could see a man swimming; all around him, through the clouded glass walls of the enclosure, a dark line of trees began, trees that stretched toward the road-less north, dark limbs of conifers, white bark of birches, their leaves golden now in the last light. The man was swimming laps, his orange trunks low on his hips. He turned his head toward the door and looked at them, his expression surprised. Then Cory heard a sound like a firecracker. The man's body arced up from the water, arms outspread as if he'd risen at the crest of a butterfly stroke. The firecracker went off again. Cory turned in the direction of the sound. Roxanne was holding a pistol. The man's body fell forward then, arms limp.

Then Roxanne pushed Cory along, jabbing her with the pistol. It was as if Cory were dreaming, and in the dream, she understood they were returning to the lobby where there was still no one at the front desk. Roxanne opened a door Cory hadn't noticed before, and they stepped into a room that was dark except for windows joining the room to the hot spring pool. The dead man's body was no longer visible on the surface.

Roxanne flipped a light switch. At her direction Cory poured two shot glasses of peppermint schnapps. They sat at the mirrored bar, Roxanne resting her elbows on the nicked counter.

"I've been drinking this stuff since I was in junior high," Roxanne said. "You're not much older than that."

Cory looked at the drink in front of her.

Roxanne gestured with the pistol. "Try some," she said in a friendly way. "I don't like to drink alone."

Cory sipped her drink, but it burned her throat, and she gagged.

Roxanne slipped her pistol into her bag. "I'm not going to

force you." She motioned toward the bar, the chipped polish on her nails reddening the air. "You can have something else."

Cory thought of ripping the bag from Roxanne's shoulder. Roxanne wasn't much bigger than Cory, but her stomach bulged slightly over her belt. The silver buckle was shaped like the head of a wide-nostrilled horse, its ear penetrating the folds of Roxanne's stomach.

"The thing is, you don't want anything else. Do you?" Roxanne asked.

Cory hesitated, putting her hands to her forehead, then pressing her fingers against her eyes as if to shut out the image of Roxanne. She tried to still the trembling of her hands, then thought of a cigarette. She said, "Can I smoke?" When Roxanne nodded, Cory reached for the pack in the pocket of the blue work shirt she'd taken from Guy's drawer. After Cory lit up, Roxanne shook several cigarettes from the pack onto the counter and began to smoke one after another. She kept dipping her free hand inside the shoulder bag, Cory guessed to touch her pistol. The afternoon light slanted through the spruces on the other side of the pool. The temperature was dropping. If the sky remained clear, the Northern Lights might be visible during the night, a time Cory had planned to spend in a room here at the lodge, celebrating the fact that she'd gotten as far away from Guy as possible. Looking at the map as she marked her route, she had thought he'd never find her at the end of an unpaved road in Alaska's interior.

The night before, she'd been in an overpriced Fairbanks motel with dirty carpets and a pay television, using what was left of the money she'd taken from Guy's wallet. Through the papery walls she could hear a baby wailing, and it made her think about the sounds coming out of her own mouth when Guy slapped her. At first it hadn't been bad because they couldn't afford much liquor, but when the work picked up he was drunk all the time. In the end, he'd broken her nose, beating her face against the floor.

This morning's first light had felt good after the dinginess of the motel. It warmed the highway pavement as she walked out, looking for a ride. There was a sky so blue it seemed unreal, like the sky in a magazine ad. She took the weather as a sign of good luck. The woman in the black Buick pulled over right away—another piece of luck—and Cory ignored the woman's wild-eyed look because she was ready for things to change.

They talked about the feeling they got driving through the forests where the gravel road tunneled through the bush, nothing human around. Roxanne kept saying, "There's no getting further than this," and Cory assumed she was talking about the way the wilderness blocked them in on all sides, so thick with the sameness of trees and brush Cory wouldn't have trusted herself to hike a hundred yards without getting lost.

When Cory asked what brought Roxanne to Alaska, she tossed her lighted cigarette out the open window. "Let's just say I joined the fucking funeral."

That made Cory think of the highway to Alaska—nothing more, in some places, than a two-lane gravel road; just inside the Canadian border there'd been a long line of cars, stalled because a bridge was out. She'd stood under the overhang of McDevitt's Gulf Services, the only place within thirty miles to offer diesel, repairs, and a 24-seat licensed cafe, and watched as the drivers turned on their headlights and started their engines in the dusk. The man who picked her up then, an insurance broker from LA, said, "I'm just going up to Anchorage to be nosy."

He wanted to know where she was from and where she was headed, glancing at her in a way that meant trouble. Cory lit a cigarette and looked out the window.

"I'm not much of a talker," she said.

He put his arm on the seat behind her. "Maybe you're a doer."

Cory picked tobacco from her tongue, then tightened her jaws and giggled. For a few hours she could play this game, humor the man if it would get her from one place to another.

Two car salesmen from Anchorage had driven her toward Fairbanks in a black TransAm, rifles propped in the back. They tried to frighten her with talk of grizzlies, but she just looked out the window at the low, treed terrain, the distant Denali barely visible behind clouds.

"A guy got ate up in Tok this year," said the one in the passenger seat. He wore a red baseball cap and drank whiskey from a bottle in a paper bag.

"You could end up like that tourist from New York." The driver's gold ring caught the light so that its reflection spotted the ceiling, and he gave off the sweet lime scent of aftershave. "They found his tent all tore up and his boot down the trail."

"Yessir," said the baseball cap, leering at Cory. "This country..."

* * *

"Why did you shoot that man? What did he do to you?" Cory asked, her voice breaking.

Roxanne's face reddened. When she spoke, her voice was low. "I knew him as well as I know my own brother. I know all of them. I know what they want and I know what they dream about and I know what they think of us."

"But what did he do?"

"Who cares?" Roxanne swiveled to face Cory and leaned close. "I been knocked around all my life. I don't mean to be knocked around no more. All I want now," she said, putting a finger against Cory's chest, "is a witness. Somebody to say,

'Roxanne did this,' or 'Roxanne did that.'" She stood up and walked behind Cory, where she played with the end of Cory's braid. "I want all those sons-of-bitches to hear my name. I want them to think it could have been them. I want them to wonder, 'Why was I spared?'" Her voice rose triumphantly.

The end of Roxanne's cigarette glowed red the way Guy's had when he held it to Cory's nipple. That last bad time, liquored up, he'd called her a whore. Maybe she was a whore. Her mother had said so, waving her painted nails and gazing out from beneath her plucked eyebrows in the trailer at the logging camp. After Cory's father died, her mother had gone to the Pentecostal Church and the revivals, looking for a man. She said Cory'd gotten too big for her britches ever since she started her period, Cory was really the only cross she had to bear.

For Cory, there'd been the preacher's son and the boy at the revival and then a man old enough to be her grandfather, one of the elders. It was flattering that they wanted her, and she liked the sex, but she didn't like the way they looked at her when they were finished, like they saw something that, once they were satisfied, they couldn't stand. She did get a kick out of watching their public confessions, though, knowing what was left out.

Guy had picked her up in his eighteen-wheeler when she was hitch-hiking. It was a relief to be around somebody who could joke and curse. At the beginning, he took her out in the woods for picnics and over to Riley's Barbeque for beers. When he heard her complain about her mother, he said the only way to get rid of her bad feelings was to get out of the situation that caused them.

For awhile after they moved in together, he drove the truck long hours and came home too tired to do anything more than eat and sleep. When she got bored and complained, the bad things began—a hard slap on her ass in front of his friends, a wrench of her neck with his hand wrapped in her long hair as they were making love. He'd come on sweet, kissing her, then his face would change and he'd start slapping, raising red welts on her skin.

"Try to get away and I'll kill you," he told her. "Wherever you go, I'll track you down."

* * *

Roxanne pulled hard on Cory's braid, stretching her neck so far back that Cory could hardly speak. Finally Cory choked out the words, "All right." When Roxanne let go of her, Cory emptied the glass.

Roxanne nodded. "You do that. You celebrate. It isn't every day a person hands you a purpose in life." She straddled the stool at the counter. "Know why I picked you?"

Cory shook her head.

"I could see you wouldn't be the type to interfere. You'd just stand and watch, like in there." She waved a hand toward the pool. "There's nothing to you." She swiveled her stool so that she could lean back against the bar.

Cory started to pour herself another drink. On the road she'd refused liquor. The hitching itself kept her numb. Outside the windows of car after car, the land moved like a TV picture. Cory watched the high prairies of Alberta pushing up against the Canadian Rockies, the long unbroken stretches of forests in British Columbia darkening the foothills, the glaciers of the Yukon melting into muddy rivers that carried whole trees downstream. There was always a blur funneling past on either side of the closed windows.

She reached for the bottle, but Roxanne grabbed her wrist. "You had enough. You got to be able to tell the story." Roxanne looked at herself in the mirror, arranging her hair with her fingers. "Don't make me sound like some dog," she said. She raised her voice then as if Cory had been arguing with her. "There's been people to call me pretty. Of course if I'd been prettier, maybe I could have been famous another way." She gestured to the left of the bar where a 1929 calendar pictured a flapper who held a bottle of Royal Crown Cola as if it were a priceless object, her lips pursed.

"Or if I'd been smart..." Roxanne directed her comments to the mirror. She shook her head. "Don't think I ever met anybody smart." She turned to Cory. "How about you?"

Cory thought of the dead man's round wire-rimmed glasses resting on the edge of the pool. She nodded toward his body. "Maybe he was."

Roxanne snorted. "He was there for me to shoot at. That wasn't smart."

Cory rested her forehead in her hand, and Roxanne leaned back against the counter. "At least I got a plan," she said. "What about you?"

Cory shuddered, fingering the broken hump of her nose.

Roxanne slapped a hand on the counter, loud as a pistol shot, so that Cory jumped. "You tell them to go fuck themselves!" She took the gun out of her bag and pointed it at Cory's heart. She closed one eye, aiming. "I can see the bull's eye."

Cory stiffened, panicking, before she remembered to look into the distance again, not to think. She saw the surface of the pool through the glass window and beyond it the clouded walls. It was dark outside. She could no longer make out the trees or the mountains. She inhaled deeply.

Roxanne lowered the pistol, grinning. "You're gonna tell them I was pretty, aren't you?"

Cory looked at Roxanne's stiffened hair, her thick mascara and caked-on rouge.

Roxanne's eyes turned bright and hard. "If you're pretty, you can kick ass, because men will do anything for you. But if you're a dumb-ass drooling drunk . . ." She pointed the pistol toward Cory. "Bang, bang." She laughed softly.

Cory felt light-headed. She dug her fingernails into her palm to try to keep herself from passing out.

Roxanne leaned close, putting a hand on Cory's cheek. "You think I done a mean thing," she said. "You think my plan stinks, don't you?" She pointed toward the pool. "Why do you think that man was here all alone? How many people did he screw to get the place?" She stood up, waving the pistol, and pulled Cory from the stool by one arm. Then she pushed Cory ahead. "Go on. Let's go look at him again."

They went through the door to the pool as they had before, except that this time Roxanne had locked her arm in Cory's.

"From here I can't tell whether I done a mean thing or not," Roxanne said. She got the long-handled net from a place where it hung on the wall, and used the pole end to work the body closer to the edge of the pool, where she turned it over with her hands. When Cory glanced down, she saw that the man's eyes and mouth were open just as they'd been when she and Roxanne first entered, but now his face was expressionless, and it floated a few inches under the water. Cory looked away. The man had had no idea what was coming. But what if Roxanne was right, what if the man had screwed someone over, or what if he'd been like Guy, beating up someone like Cory, someone who'd be grateful he was dead? Cory's hands moved to her stomach. The liquor had left a strange taste in her mouth.

Roxanne looked up at her. "Well, he don't look unhappy to me. What do you think?"

The pool was lit from below. Ripples circled outward from the body, reflecting on the walls and ceiling. Roxanne's forehead shone, but her eyes and mouth hollowed in the half-light. Suddenly she flipped the pistol in one hand and offered it, butt-first, to Cory.

Cory's throat burned and her arms felt heavy, too heavy to move.

Roxanne turned the pistol around again so that the barrel was pointed toward Cory. She cocked the hammer.

"Wait," Cory said, holding up her hands in front of her face.

"What for?" Roxanne waved her arms to indicate the dark line of trees beyond the glass room. "Don't you think this is where you belong? Weren't you heading for the end of the road?"

"No."

Roxanne twirled the pistol again and held it out. "You want to live, you have to kill me first. You got to the count of three."

Cory took the pistol. She felt for the hammer.

"One," Roxanne said.

Cory pulled back the hammer.

"Shoot me here." Roxanne pointed to her chest. "That way you won't mess up my face. Two."

Cory held the pistol with both hands, aiming for the place where Roxanne had pointed.

Roxanne slipped her belt from around her waist. "No use getting this messed up. Here." She flung it on the floor toward Cory. "The buckle ought to be worth something. It's real silver. That and the car are all I got. You can have the pistol, too, if you want it." She ducked her head. "You probably won't. Shit." She blinked rapidly.

For a moment there was nothing but the sound of lapping water. Then Roxanne said, "If you don't kill me by three I'll have to kill you. That was the way we set it up."

"We don't have to do it that way," Cory said faintly.

Roxanne closed her eyes, then opened them and looked at Cory with something like longing. "Soon as you took that pistol you grew tits. You should of been holding that pistol all your life. It almost makes me want to change the plan, seeing how good you look.

"When I was your age if somebody'd done for me what I'm doing for you I would of built a shrine to her. I would of put flowers on her grave everyday. Killing an asshole," she nodded toward the dead man, "and making the rest of them afraid."

"I didn't ask you to do anything," Cory said. "I didn't want you to kill anybody, and I don't want to kill you."

"You're doing me a favor," Roxanne said flatly. She rubbed her nose with the back of her hand. "I been like you most of my life. Letting other people take me for a ride. Letting them leave me off wherever they felt like it. You were already tired of it or you wouldn't of been here."

Cory's arms ached from holding up the pistol. She began to lower it. "How do you know that?"

Roxanne watched the pistol. "I ain't said three yet, but when I do you better lift that thing back up."

Cory nodded.

"If you don't I'll put you in the water just like I put him." She nodded toward the pool. "You're either the right woman for the job or you ain't."

Cory said, "I'm the right woman. I mean—"

Roxanne laughed. "See? I'm watching you change, and I'm the one doing it. I'm making you into somebody." She laughed again, softly, then said, "Three."

Cory lifted the pistol as if she were aiming for Roxanne, but when she made a sudden, jerking motion, meaning to throw the pistol into the pool, Roxanne lunged, catching her arm. The pistol dropped to the tile floor. The two of them grappled, the pistol sliding between their hands as one reached out and the other knocked it loose, one grabbed for it and the other kicked it away. Roxanne was so close she was breathing on Cory's neck, and Cory could smell her hairspray and the tobacco and schnapps on her breath. The smells sickened her like the thick exhaust of cars heading north. Cory's throat felt tight, as if she were suffocating, as if the trees outside were pressing on the glass walls. Cory pushed Roxanne toward the pool. Roxanne came at her again, but Cory had the pistol now, and she aimed the muzzle toward Roxanne's chest. Roxanne walked right into it, then shoved Cory; she was shoving at Cory grinning—little pushes on Cory's shoulders that moved Cory backwards a step at a time until her back was pressed against the wall. Roxanne reached for the pistol with the same motion a grown-up uses to snatch a toy from a child, but Cory pulled the trigger, then kept firing into the air toward the place where Roxanne had been.

AMERICAN PRIMITIVE

IN THE CAR ON THE WAY UP INTO THE MOUNTAINS, Betsy's father called her stupid again. She had tried to be good, but when they rounded the curves, she couldn't help sliding into her brother Logan. Logan rested his knees against the seat in front of him, wedging himself. He wore a crewcut that made his head look square and had long, skinny arms and legs like a spider's. But he was stronger than a spider. When Betsy slid into him, he pushed her back, hard. That made her cry. Finally her father pulled the car off by a market, turned around in his seat, and shook his head. "Stupid." Under the thatched roof, toward the front of the market, hung a row of shrunken heads. He pointed a finger at them. "You want to wind up like that?"

"Please," her mother Alice said. "You're scaring Betsy." She opened a compact and refreshed her lipstick.

Her father had called Betsy stupid lots of times, but it still hurt her feelings. She wasn't really scared, as her mother seemed to think. She just felt dumb. At the dinner table last night, he'd called her stupid. Now she was stupid again. Last night all she'd done was ask if she could talk to the Filipino men she saw outside the compound gate. Her father had said no, she wasn't to speak to those men, they just wanted what the Americans had—they were hungry.

"Should we bring them some food?"

"No, honey. They're not hungry for food. They're hungry for what we have." They sat at the dining table. The maids were in the kitchen. He gestured toward the silverware, the furniture, the chandelier hanging from the ceiling.

"But they're nice. They always wave at me." She had thought it was good of her to care.

"Don't be stupid," her father had said. "You watch Uncle Bob."

On "The Uncle Bob Show," a man with a blonde crewcut and dark-framed heavy glasses always started by holding up pictures of American children who had been kidnapped. She understood that American children would bring bigger ransoms than Filipinos, but she hadn't thought the men outside the gates meant any harm. They always smiled when they saw her looking at them through the window of the school bus, as if she were special.

"Maybe we'll all feel better if we stretch our legs," Betsy's mother said.

They got out of the car and went into the market, where the people spoke a language Betsy didn't understand. She'd learned some Tagalog from the maids and some Spanish at the American School, but all she could do in either language was count to ten. Betsy's father had a firm hold on her hand. His palm was big and dry. Today he didn't have on his uniform, but people stepped aside for him anyway. He was bigger and handsomer than most. Betsy's mother draped an arm around Logan's shoulders and glided next to Betsy's father, the same way she did when they had a cocktail party and she moved from group to group. She wore pale blue shorts and a white linen embroidered blouse. Betsy straightened up, trying to walk like her mother, but she was stopped by the proximity of the shrunken heads, on the wall to her left now, just past a table of carved wooden bowls. Her father tugged at her hand. "Come on, babe, they're not real."

Betsy stared. "What are they made of?"

"Wood and horse hair, probably. They're not real," he said again.

After they'd returned to the car and started up the mountain again, her father said in a disgusted voice, "These people are throwbacks."

* * *

When they got to the cottage they were renting in Baguio, Betsy walked onto the lawn, pulling her sweater tight. It was chillier here than in Quezon City. The air was so cool and pure it almost hurt her to breathe. At the edge of the lawn, the land fell away into a tangled ravine. Distant slopes rose above it, covered with the same color green that made Betsy want to close her eyes, that was almost too much for her. Mists formed a solid bank like sea foam beneath the slopes.

How could there be headhunters in a place like this? In movies they were always in hot jungles, not up in mountains so high they made you think of God. Betsy's parents didn't go to church, but behind their house on the compound was a small chapel where Betsy took piano lessons. The door to the chapel was unlocked all the time, so she could practice there between lessons. She liked going into the building alone. She always opened the door slowly, afraid she might interrupt someone who was praying, but most of the time the chapel was empty except for a feeling. The feeling waited for her. It was like being scared and happy at the same time. She got the feeling when she closed the door behind her and listened to the quiet and looked

up at Jesus on the stained glass window stretching out his hands
to the little children. All the children were beautiful and smiling. No wonder Jesus loved them so much. When she sat down
at the piano to practice, she prayed that God would forgive her
for filling His house with so many wrong notes. It was a good
thing Daddy didn't hear her. He would probably say she was
making his head hurt. They were on this vacation, Mommy had
said, because Daddy needed a rest. His head hurt a lot. At night
sometimes Betsy could hear him yelling at her mother. Once
she'd heard a glass break. The next morning her mother's face
was cut. When Betsy asked what happened, her mother said
she'd had an accident. She'd had another one about a week ago.
Betsy saw a big ugly bruise on her mother's arm. Maybe Mommy
needed a vacation, too.

Logan came up beside her, his skinny legs pale in the deep-
ening shadows.

Betsy whispered, "What do you think? Do you think they're
really out there?"

"No," Logan said. But he looked alert, his fists clenched and
slightly raised. A few minutes ago, he'd called her a baby for
being afraid of the headhunters. She'd run into the cottage
because she'd heard something in the woods. It sounded like a
bird call, but maybe that was the noise the headhunters used
when they wanted to signal each other. She imagined them cir-
cling her in the dark woods, raising their spears; so she ran.
Inside, her parents had their feet propped on the window sill.
They were drinking martinis. Betsy buried her face in her mother's lap.

"What a baby," Logan had said.

"I'm not a baby," Betsy had replied.

"Go outside with your little sister and protect her from the
headhunters," Bill had said. "That'll keep you busy."

So Logan had followed her. For some reason Logan wasn't

afraid of the headhunters. Betsy knew what he was afraid of: the dogs' heads in the market. When he had seen them, Betsy had heard him gasp, then watched as he turned away, closing his eyes. They'd had a dog in the States—Butterscotch, a cocker spaniel. They'd had her since she was a puppy. Sometimes she slept with Logan. Often, even though their parents had forbidden it, Betsy saw Logan feed the dog under the dinner table. The dog went everywhere with him—to the neighbors' houses, on bike rides. They'd left her with their grandparents. Betsy and Logan both missed her. Betsy couldn't imagine eating her.

"I don't think I could cut off somebody's head," Betsy said.

"I could," Logan replied. "I'd sneak up with the other head-hunters and we'd surround the enemy and whoosh." He swiped the air with his hand. Then he narrowed his eyes and stared into the forest in the direction Betsy was looking. The shadows had deepened between the trees.

"You'd be as easy to catch as a gecko," he said to his sister. Geckos were the lizards that clung stupidly to the walls of their house in the compound. Logan could catch them by grabbing their tails, but when he did, the tails detached and the head and body escaped.

Betsy whimpered, a puppyish sound.

"Don't worry," Logan said. "I'll protect you."

By the time their mother called them in for dinner, it was almost completely dark. The forest was blacker than the open area around the cottages; it looked like the mouth of a cave. A few stars appeared in the sky. Betsy had taken Logan's hand and would not let it go as they walked around the periphery of the empty cottages. By the weekend, there might be other military families here, but Daddy had taken his vacation in the middle of the week to avoid the crowd.

"If there were an invasion now," Logan said, "it'd be all up to me and Dad to protect you and Mom."

"Just like General MacArthur."

In school they had learned that Gen. Douglas MacArthur had rescued the Filipinos from the Japanese after they invaded during World War II. Betsy imagined the Japanese flocking to the ocean like ants, plunging into the sea foam trying to escape while MacArthur stood like a giant on the headland. When the children played war with their friends on the compound, the boys flipped coins to see who would be Gen. MacArthur. After the Americans captured the Japanese, they put them in prison in Mark Sippowitz's sky fort. Unlike the Japanese, the Americans were kind to their prisoners. They allowed the girls to bring the prisoners lunch. But when the Japanese caught the Americans, they kept them in cardboard boxes Doug Muenster had in his clubhouse and pretended to push splinters under their nails. The girls pleaded for the Americans' lives, but the Japanese just laughed at them, saying, "They ah the enemy. We wrike to tleat them bahd."

When Betsy looked at the pictures in her history book, she noticed that in addition to actually winning, the Americans also looked like winners. They were taller and whiter than the Japanese, and their uniforms, without the red zeros, looked less sinister. Her father, in his khaki shorts and green golf shirt, blonde hair cut short like Logan's, was handsome, too. Weekend days, he got out his putter and showed Logan and Betsy how to hit a golf ball into a cup. Sometimes they went swimming at the compound pool. Daddy threw her up in the air, making her squeal, then caught her as she splashed down in the pool. Lately Logan and Daddy were helping Betsy learn how to ride her bike, taking turns holding the seat while she wobbled down the street. Their mother would applaud as Betsy went by, encouraging all of them. But when Daddy drank martinis, his voice got louder, his face meaner. He picked on Logan or Betsy or their mother, criticizing the way they ate or sat or talked, but usually their mother said, "Honestly, Bill. What do you need?"

Sometimes that made him angry and quiet. He stabbed at his food with his fork. But once he had put his big hands on the table, palms down, and stuck his upper teeth out over his bottom lip as if he were a vampire. "I doon't know, Aleeece. I moost be hoongry."

He had a way of grabbing Betsy's mother when she was least expecting it, pushing his body into hers from behind. It made Betsy nervous; she thought her mother seemed frightened. Sometimes she tugged on her father, saying, "Let Mommy go," but he just laughed and squeezed her mother tighter and said, "I'm not hurting her, babe. I'm just reminding her where she belongs."

Once he had grabbed Betsy like that, too. When she screamed, her mother came into the room, and her father let her go. He put his hands out to the sides, shrugging his shoulders. "What? I was just playing."

"I hope Marcos can figure out how to get these people organized," her father was saying when Betsy and Logan walked in. Betsy knew Marcos was the new President of the Philippines. Once, her parents had been invited to the Palace to meet him. They'd shaken his hand.

"See any headhunters?" her father asked.

Betsy shook her head.

"You know," said her father, "they don't take heads anymore, unless you take one of theirs first, but they used to."

Alice sat up in her chair and touched her husband's arm. "Bill, stop."

He looked at the children, then back at his wife. "It was especially bad during the Jap occupation." He sighed, shaking his head. "But even a headhunting expedition takes some organization, and the Phil Navy ain't got that."

"What did they do during the Jap-oc-cu-pa-tion?" Betsy asked.

Her father started to speak, but her mother said, "Now hush."

When they sat down at the table, everyone was quiet. Betsy's stomach cramped. Logan glanced at his father.

"What's everybody so glum about? Even the air's better up here." Alice tossed her hair back, smiling.

Bill took a drink of his martini, then shoveled a fork full of macaroni into his mouth.

"Are you going to play golf tomorrow?" Logan asked. "Can I ride on the cart?"

"Maybe," his father said.

"Me too?" Betsy asked.

Her father looked at his plate, his jaw working furiously.

"Let Daddy eat," Alice said. "He had a long drive today."

"You know, in some ways the headhunter's ethic makes sense," Bill said. He drew his finger across his neck. "A head for a head." He pointed across the table at Alice. "Not a free ride like the one we're giving."

"'An eye for an eye makes the whole world blind,'" said Alice. "Gandhi said that."

"The guy was assassinated. By his own kind yet."

"If we go on the cart tomorrow, can I try hitting some, too?" Logan asked.

Bill put down his fork. "You know, even though the head-hunters aren't taking heads anymore, they do still take children."

"What for?" Logan mumbled, looking down at his hamburger.

"To sell."

"Bill," his wife said. "Honestly."

"These kids aren't scared. Come on. They belong to me." He raised his hands up like claws and grimaced. "What'd you kids see out there? Any ooga-boogas?"

Betsy looked down at her plate, tapping her sneakers together.
"Nothing," Logan said.

Alice's lipstick was smeared. She smiled loosely, lifting her
martini from the table. "Bill—"

Logan picked up his hamburger. His father pursed his lips
and drank. Betsy had both hands around her cup of milk. Her
father put his glass down.

"Maybe Betsy doesn't believe me," he said in an accusing
voice. "Maybe she's scared. Maybe she'd rather be home playing
with her dollies."

"No I wouldn't." Her hands shook as she put her milk down
and picked up her hamburger. She chewed, but her stomach was
churning. It felt like she was still riding in the station wagon on
the twisting road up into the mountains. The meat tasted leath-
ery, like the skin on the shrunken heads.

"You eat that," her father said in a loud voice. "You eat it
now or you're going to get a spanking."

Betsy gagged with her mouth closed, praying to Jesus, trying
not to spit out the food. She tried to convince herself that the
meat was from a cow. Tried to forget the sensation of movement
around the curves, sliding around in the back seat; tried to put
the shrunken heads out of her mind and tell herself the faces she
thought she saw in the woods were only in her imagination. She
looked at her mother, but her mother had the false smile she got
when she wanted everything to be all right, and she looked at
Logan, but he had his eyes shut tight, and she was afraid to look
at her father, so she just looked into her plate, at the bitten hamburger, at the ketchup oozing from beneath the bun, and it made
her think of the blood dripping from the hands of Christ in the
picture Bible and from beneath his crown of thorns, and the
blood that would spurt from the neck of the victim when the
headhunters lopped off their heads, and the blood from her
scraped knee when she fell off her bike onto the road, and the

hamburger filled her mouth like flesh—it was the flesh of an animal—and there was nothing she could do about it, the nausea took over, and though she put her hands to her mouth, the vomit came, overflowing onto her plate, onto the table.

"Ohhh," Logan moaned, putting his hands to his mouth. He got out of his chair and backed up from the table.

Tears streamed down Betsy's face. "I'm sorry," she said. "I'm sorry."

Her father sat without moving. "I told you to eat your dinner," he said in a low, menacing tone. "I told you to eat your dinner, and you turned it into that."

Logan looked at his plate.

Alice's face was white. She slid her chair back from the table and got up and stood behind Betsy, rubbing her back. "She's sick, that's all. You can't punish her for that."

"She's not sick. She's pretending to be sick so she doesn't have to eat. I work hard to put this food on the table." He stood up, unbuckled his belt, and took it off. He ran the leather between his hands "She's ungrateful, just like the fucking Filipinos. Do something good for someone and they barf it back in your face." He started toward Betsy.

"Bill, don't," his wife said. "We're all on vacation. This is supposed to be a vacation." She wiped Betsy's mouth with a napkin, lifted her up and pushed her toward the bathroom, then turned to look at her husband. "Bill—"

He grabbed her by one arm, raising the belt with the other. She raised her arms as if to fend him off.

"Mommy!" Betsy screamed.

Bill looked at Betsy in the doorway and then at Logan who stood at the table gripping the back of his chair.

Alice caught her breath. "You're drunk. You're drunk and you don't know what you're doing. Go outside." She motioned for the door. "Why don't you just go outside and take a walk.

Clear your head."

He looked at his wife again, then at his hand on her arms. He let it slip down, then clenched and released his fists.

"Logan, open the door for your father," his mother said.

Logan didn't move.

"You can't kick me out," Bill said. "I'll go if I'm not wanted, but you can't kick me out." He looked like he was going to cry.

"Daddy," Betsy said. She looked at Alice. "Don't make him go away."

"All I'm saying is you need a little walk," said Betsy's mother. She was rubbing her arm where her husband had gripped it. "I'll make some coffee."

"Betsy wants me to stay," Bill said.

"Betsy's a little girl," Alice said. "What do you expect?"

Bill pointed a finger at his wife. "You're a fucking bitch," he said in a low, menacing voice. "You send me out into that jungle, don't expect me to come back."

* * *

From the lower bunk, Betsy could see the square of window. Her father was out there somewhere, walking around. Headhunters could be watching him from the woods. Logan was silent above her, but she knew he wasn't asleep. Their mother had sent them to bed. For awhile Betsy had listened to the clink of dishes as her mother cleaned up the table and washed the plates. She would have had to wipe up Betsy's vomit with paper towels. Betsy couldn't believe she had thrown up. It was awful, the awfulest thing she'd ever done. She was bad, she was evil, she prayed to God to forgive her.

"Betsy?" Logan said.

"Yeah."

"Did you hear that?"

"What?"

"I thought I heard Mom lock the door. If she locks the door, how's Dad going to get back in?"

Betsy strained her eyes, looking into the dark beyond the window for her father's shape, or the shapes of headhunters. The sound of crying came from the other room. The bedsprings creaked above her as Logan turned over.

"He shouldn't have tried to punish you for throwing up," Logan said. "He shouldn't have grabbed Mom."

Betsy's mother stood in the doorway. Her eyes were swollen and red. "You kids try and get some sleep."

"Where's Daddy?" Betsy asked.

"How's he going to get back in?" Logan said. "I heard you lock the door."

His mother said nothing.

"Mommy, what about the headhunters? Aren't the head-hunters going to get him?"

Just then a face appeared at the window, a face so savage and strange that they all screamed. The face snarled; then hands appeared beside it, clawing on the window as if it were trying to come in.

"Bill." The sound came from Alice's throat as if she were strangling.

He put his hands out to either side, palms up. He said something, but they couldn't hear him through the window.

He was smiling, and once again he looked familiar, but Betsy remembered the way he had come toward her with the belt, then gripped her mother's arm; she thought of the ugly words he had said. Her father was at her window, big and hand-some. In a way, she wanted to go up to the window and put her hand to the glass, but there was something about him that still wasn't right—a look in his eyes like the looks of the Filipino men outside the compound gate, the men Daddy had said she couldn't talk to. Betsy turned over. She lay with Logan above her and her mother in the doorway. She held her eyelids closed, praying to Jesus that everything would be all right, and pretended to sleep.

WIND ACROSS THE BREAKS

I PUT THE BABY SWING, BABY BLANKET, stuffed animals and toys in Nathan's room. Then I let in the dog. She'd been exiled into the yard after the baby came, since Sarah had read a few newspaper accounts of jealous pets harming small children. The dog was a golden retriever named Amber who liked to lick you in the face. Sarah didn't think that would be too good for the baby either. Amber bounded in, grinning like dogs do, her tail slapping the furniture, knocking down the Polaroid of newborn Nathan that Sarah had already framed. I stroked Amber's head, then told her to lie down. She went right to her spot in the middle of the living room floor and sacked out, rolling onto her back and twisting with her paws in the air, letting out happy grunts, then collapsing onto her side with her legs straight out.

Through the sliding glass door, I looked out over the back pasture. Snow made everything bright on the treeless hills. The snow wasn't too deep; I could see the wheat stubble poking up at the back of our fenced pasture on the hill that rose behind the house. Beyond that hill, Mule Deer Mountain's slopes were dark with pines. We'd be cross-country skiing there again, Sarah and I, once this crisis with Nathan was over. We'd seen a moose along the trail last time, about two months before Nathan was born. Sarah, too big to fit in her own ski overalls, wore mine. Her long braid, thick as my wrist, hung to her waist, and her cheeks flushed with the exertion. She'd taken off her wool ski cap and stuck it in the belt of her fanny pack. She had freckles, cornflower eyes fringed by pale lashes, and a pert, turned-up nose. Most people thought of her as cute in a tomboy kind of way, but to me "cute" always meant small, as in petite, and Sarah wasn't small. She was five feet ten inches—big for a woman, but just right for me; I was six foot three.

Ever since I'd known Sarah—about ten years—she'd been an athlete: triathlon, mostly. But her pregnancy had made her awkward. Though we stayed on the flattest trails, she had trouble keeping her balance that day and fell right on her nose as we came down a slight incline. I saw it happen, the slow wobble forward, the way she protected her belly by folding in half as best she could, pushing her head forward to take the impact. It didn't surprise me that she thought to protect the baby—she knows what to do with her body instinctively—but I skied back anyway to be sure she was all right.

"I'll have to be more careful," she said. "I wasn't thinking." She brushed the snow off her front, then rested a hand on her belly. I started to go on, but didn't hear Sarah behind me, so looked back to see if she was following. She stood with her eyes closed, breathing deeply, tears running down her face.

When Sarah gets frustrated, I always get angry. I try to be patient—and sometimes I am; sometimes I just hold her and rub her back and tell her how much I love her. But other times I want to shake her, shake her until I shake out all the self-pity. When I feel this way, I think it's just better to leave, so I skied ahead.

Sarah followed me in her own good time. That seemed to be

all right. When we do fight over something, it's usually because one of us got in too close, not because of our distance. We're married, yes; we've lived together for five years, yes; but we're separate, too. When we go camping together, for instance, I'll get up before Sarah does and go fishing and maybe not see her again until dinnertime. Even if I come back for lunch, she's usually off by herself somewhere, collecting rocks. Sarah's a geologist. I teach Shop or, as they call it now, Industrial Arts.

With our two careers and our hobbies, it was difficult to decide we would have a baby, and though we are intelligent enough people, and had made a well-informed decision to become parents, Nathan's presence was a shock to us both. His crying filled every room, as relentless and wearing as the wind across the breaks. It reached even the basement, where I tried to escape in my woodshop. I whittle small animals—beavers, moose, elk, bear, whatever is native to these parts. Moving the blade along the soft wood, I imagine the animal taking shape.

I had not thought of such a thing happening with human beings—formlessness giving way to shape—until Sarah became pregnant. Hearing the heartbeat through the obstetrician's stethoscope before Sarah's belly even began to swell, then seeing the cloudy limbs on the Ultrasound picture, I had the same deep feeling I used to get as a child looking up at the stars, as if I were both as large as the universe and as insignificant as a speck of dust. It's hard for me to express how I felt when Nathan was finally born. When I close my eyes I can still see his little round head protruding from my wife's dark-furred vagina, his limbs springing free of her, then his small, sharp wise-looking face taking in his new surroundings. I couldn't stop touching him, even after they put him on Sarah's bare chest; it was as if I had to convince myself that he was real, that what I'd just seen really had happened. After the nurses cleaned up the baby and Sarah, and we had Nathan in the hospital room, Sarah held him all night, and I sat in the chair beside them, one hand on Sarah's arm. I told her I had never been so much in love with her, and it was true, every word.

Now it was Sarah who sat in the chair next to Nathan. He lay naked and unconscious on a small bed enclosed by plastic. An IV was hooked to his tiny arm. A blindfold protected his eyes from the light that would, eventually we hoped, reduce the bilirubin levels. A tube fixed around his penis led to a bag which, once he was rehydrated, would collect his urine. A monitor on his chest measured his heartbeat. He had dropped from his birth weight of six pounds to five. He looked like a preemie.

The doctor, a heavyset man with small eyes, had shaken our hands after he'd examined Nathan, introduced himself, and said, "He's severely jaundiced. His bilirubin level is sky high. If he wasn't so dehydrated, I'd fly him to Spokane for a transfusion. We've got fluids going into him and the UV light on to reduce the bili levels. We've done all we can do. Now it's in God's hands."

We'd been calling the nurses at the hospital every day for a week since we'd brought Nathan home, telling them our baby was crying. They'd said, "Babies cry." We'd been checking the diapers, but they were the absorbent, disposable kind, and we didn't know what a wet one felt like. Finally, the morning we'd brought Nathan in, he had stopped crying. He lay on the bed without moving. He looked parched, like a very old man; I realized this in hindsight—that he was, in fact, dehydrated, but I didn't know what was wrong then.

Sarah sat in the metal chair next to the incubator and looked at Nathan. She didn't stir when I said I was going home to feed the dog. She said, "All right."

* * *

I whittled on a mallard. It was giving me trouble. I went slowly, carving tiny pieces. The mute heads of the animals I had shot hung on the wall—a deer, an antelope, a bear. Somehow those big heads seemed to be looking at me with sympathetic eyes as if to say, "You killed us, but we understand." I kept a coyote pelt next to my workbench so I could stroke it when my hands started to hurt from the effort of carving. I put down the mallard and ran my hands over the pelt, looking out the high narrow window at the bright white of the landscape. The wind rattled the glass. Upstairs it would be louder, since there were more windows. I'd hear the high whistle of it moving around the house.

* * *

When I got back to the hospital, Sarah was lying down on a bench in the hallway outside Nathan's room. She wore sweat pants and an oversized flannel shirt. Her hair, loose to her waist, clung to one side of her head. Sarah's got high cheekbones and a square jaw that normally makes her look determined. But now the skin swelled around her eyes from crying and in her expression was more grief than I had ever seen in anyone. It frightened me. Though I had at first moved to hug her, I stopped myself and looked at the floor.

"They asked if I wanted to talk to a minister," she said. "Do you?"

I shook my head. I'd been annoyed when the doctor said, "It's in God's hands now," as if he were giving up his responsibility.

"Let's go home," I said.

"And leave him?" She gestured toward Nathan.

"We can't do anything for him here."

Sarah returned to Nathan's room. I followed. There was nothing in the room but Nathan, his incubator, the machines and the chair in which Sarah'd been sitting. It was a small hospital with only two rooms for Intensive Care. Tonight Nathan was the only patient. I looked at the baby. He was my son, but he seemed older than I was with that tiny, wrinkled, serious face.

"It doesn't seem fair," I said. "I should've been able to protect him at least this long."

I wanted Sarah to touch me, to say it was all right, I didn't really fail our son, but she stood apart, her shoulders hunched tightly, bent over her crossed arms as if someone had just punched her in the stomach.

She'd shown me the little white drops coming out of her nipples a few days after Nathan came home. Sarah was a small-breasted woman, and I think she'd been nervous about whether the milk would come. When it did, or anyway when she thought it had, she went around the house with her shirt unbuttoned, her breasts fuller than either of us had ever seen them. I was proud of her patience—up through the nights, hour after hour, with our son at her breasts in the rocking chair. Nathan wouldn't really suck the way I guess babies are supposed to, the way I thought came naturally. He'd try to, but then he'd turn his head and cry. It seemed he never stopped crying. When we put him in his bassinet to sleep, if his eyes were closed when we laid him down, they'd open as soon as his body felt the mattress.

Sarah drank the glasses of water, made sure to eat enough calories—the only thing she didn't get was any rest, since Nathan didn't sleep. Maybe that's why, as we found out in the hospital when they hooked Sarah up to the electric milking machine, she had no milk. They said she might have had milk earlier; the shock of hearing the baby was in critical condition might have dried up her supply. It was impossible to know. When Sarah heard this explanation she said nothing, but I know Sarah. In a race once she fell and sprained her ankle but got up and tried to make it to the finish. When she couldn't, the injury was the least of her pain. She went over the fall again and again during the weeks she was on crutches, trying to locate her mistake. In our bed late at night, her foot propped on a pillow, she went deep into her own character. "Walt," she'd said, "maybe I was just too greedy. If I hadn't been in such a hurry to push past the others into the inside lane, I wouldn't have got so tangled up."

During those weeks of Sarah's self-recriminations, I tried to talk to her with my hands, to tell her again and again that I loved her, that no mistake was too bad, that her ankle would heal and she'd win the next race. When she didn't respond, and I felt myself getting angry, I either went into my woodshop or, on the nicer days, drove down the grade to the Clearwater River. Standing in the water with my dry fly bouncing in the riffles, I thought of the way the light worked on the water and the hills; took in the smell of water and sagebrush. I imagined myself a heron standing in the shallows, sharp beak ready to stab his prey.

Finally I'd feel the tug on the line, set the hook and let the fish fight. The invisible force would race out, taking the line, then back, sometimes letting me catch a glimpse of itself as it flipped in the air, trying to shake loose; but finally I'd bring it in, its gills heaving, and surround it with my net. I'd stroke it with my fingers under the water, admiring its colors, then put the fish up on the bank and in one quick motion, stab it in the eye.

The first time Sarah ever saw me do that, she backed away. I looked up from the riverbank, where I had laid the fish aside to wash my hands. The day was cloudless and hot. We'd been drinking beer on the gravel bar, getting up once in a while to fish. When we wanted to make love, we moved into a thick grove of cottonwoods and fashioned a bed with our clothes. She was beautiful, I thought, and exciting because she was so much at home under the sky. But when I killed the fish, she turned away from me, shielding her eyes. "Jesus Christ."

* * *

Sarah saw the cleared-out living room, Amber sprawled on the carpet as she always was before Nathan was born, and she didn't say a word. I saw her pause at the closed door of Nathan's room, as if to make sense of it, before she turned to go into our own bedroom.

After we lay down together, I reached for Sarah's hand. She let me squeeze it, then pulled it away.

"He's going to be all right," I said.

"I hope so," Sarah said.

"It's not your fault."

"I should've realized it sooner." Sarah sounded like she was going to cry again, so I was glad for the darkness between us. "It was because I didn't want to seem like some hysterical mother. That's why I didn't bring him in. I didn't want the doctor to think of me like that. So Nathan might die because I didn't want some doctor to think I was a wimp."

"We're both to blame," I said. But I didn't know if I believed it. What could I do to help with breast-feeding? I thought how naturally such things came to animals and wondered—as I often did—what was the problem with human beings. I had thought Sarah was different, tougher. She could outhike most of my buddies. But I guess that had nothing to do with being a mother. "I'll call the hospital," I said. "I'll see how he is."

"No." Sarah put a hand on my arm as I reached for the phone. "I just need to think he's okay. If he's worse, I don't want to know yet." She got out of bed and unplugged the phone.

I imagined finding out in the morning that my son was dead, that he'd died by himself in an incubator. If he died we'd probably never forgive ourselves for being home while he was there by himself. Yet I lay stiffly next to my wife and listened to her breathing; neither of us moved.

After awhile, I heard Amber moan in her sleep and got up to check on her. Moonlight shone through the sliding glass doors, illuminating the piano, the coffee table with its scattered magazines, the leather chairs and couch. I'd arranged wood and newspapers in the fireplace so I could light it in the morning, but I opened the damper and lit it now. Amber opened her eyes and thumped her tail against the wood floor, then yawned and stretched and got up to lean against me. The fire crackled. I stroked Amber's head, moved away from the heat, felt the runner of the rocking chair in my back and thought of Nathan sucking on that dry breast and getting nothing, his mother giving him all she had, not realizing how little she offered. How could Sarah not have realized? Why couldn't she feel the emptiness of her own breasts? Why not notice that Nathan didn't burp or spit up like babies did who were getting what they needed? I thought of my son sucking desperately, his little eyes closed.

I went into Nathan's room, got his blanket and brought it into the living room with me. I held it to my face and breathed in my son's smell—baby powder and urine and some indefinable scent of newness. To me, I'll have to admit, Nathan had not seemed quite human. He was a miracle, I thought, in the sense that he had come alive from my sperm and Sarah's egg after the long incubation. I had my fantasies about the time he'd be old enough to go hunting and fishing with me. But also I kept imagining—even when I thought he was healthy—that Nathan would never change, that even at 21 he'd have the same solemn faraway look, and we'd have to strap him into a wheelchair to get him to sit up. It had frightened me so much that I had to wonder if, in a way, what had happened was something I had wished on him. Now, according to the doctor, if Nathan survived, brain damage really was possible.

If that did happen, maybe my son would be better off dead. What kind of life would he have otherwise—kids making fun of him, never a girlfriend, much less a wife. If he outlived us, he'd probably have to be institutionalized—and what about our lives? We'd be prisoners, in effect.

Once, Sarah and I had come across a deer hit on the highway. She was stunned but alive, her head up, eyes glazed with shock, one leg turned at an angle. Sarah bent to stroke her neck, talking gently to her, but I thought of my hunting knife in the truck and sprinted back. In my hand the leather of the sheath felt solid and important. Sarah asked me later why I hadn't asked her what she wanted to do, why I wordlessly lifted the doe's head and slit her throat.

"I don't know," I told my wife. "It was just a reflex."

She didn't help me when I gathered the deer into my arms and pitched her off the side of the road.

Amber lay her head on my lap, on the blue-and-white squares of the blanket Sarah had crocheted for the baby. The bacteria Amber might carry, might leave on Nathan's blanket, seemed unimportant now. I didn't scold her. What got you was never the thing you guarded against; it was what you didn't see—for the doe, that truck hurtling through darkness; for Nathan, our ignorance. I rubbed an end of Nathan's blanket back and forth between my hands. I closed my eyes and thought of my son just as I'd seen him last. I imagined my own life as if it were in my chest, housed there like light, and I pictured my chest opening, freeing the light that moved out our front door, down our lane, left on Third, right on Main and into the front entrance of the hospital. It moved in a beam from my chest to Nathan's. If I could hold him in that light, I thought he might live. I might sustain him even from here by the fire at home with the dog's head in my lap; even here, with my fears and doubts about what life with Nathan would be like if he recovered. I beamed the light into him until I was dizzy. It was all I could think to do for him, and it seemed as important as anything I'd ever done. I squeezed my eyes shut, concentrating on keeping my son alive, on firing my own good health into him through my brain, through my imagination which—right then—was as real to me as a rifle scope. As I aimed, I could hear nothing but the beating of my heart, the pulsing of my breath, the crackling of the fire far away, forgotten, and Sarah's approach unheard, unimagined, until she laid a hand on my arm and I opened my eyes and couldn't think who she was—only that she was in the way, blocking my shot like a hunting partner who had no sense, and I pushed her away, leaping up so fast that Amber yelped with fright. Sarah pressed herself against the wall and said, "Walt." She held her hands up as if to ward me off, but my arm moved as if by reflex, like the leg that kicks at the doctor when he strikes the knee; the momentum carried my closed fist between her upraised hands and struck her jaw, so that her head snapped to one side, knees buckling as her hands moved up to her face and she cried out.

I pulled my fist back and stepped away, putting my hands out to my sides, palms up, like a teenager in the police car's headlights saying, "I don't have a thing. I'm clean." Then I knelt beside my wife, but she said, "Get away," and flailed her arms in my direction.

I moved back. I went into the kitchen, pausing at the window. The moon had sunk and a harsh gray light shone at the edges of the horizon. The dog whined. I noticed the car keys hanging on a hook beside the sink. I put them in my pocket, closed my eyes briefly, then turned back to my wife. She still sat on the floor with her back against the wall. Her face was splotchy and red, swelling, but she had picked up Nathan's blanket and now held it against her face, as I had.

I moved toward her, but she said, "Don't touch me."

I said, "I'm sorry. I didn't mean to hit you. It was just some weird kind of reflex. I didn't mean anything." I pointed to my chin. "Hit me back." I squeezed my eyes shut. "Hit me back. Please."

She rubbed the fabric of Nathan's blanket against her jaw. Then she got up and carried the blanket out to the car. Through the window I watched her get into the passenger seat.

I looked at Amber. I said, "You can stay here."

I followed Sarah. We didn't look at each other. We didn't speak. We put on our seat belts. I don't think either of us cared right then whether we lived or died; it was just a habit, each of us pulling the buckles across to lock ourselves in place.

TOY GUNS

I THOUGHT ABOUT IT FIRST IN THE WHEATLEY TOY STORE—forty miles from the Bi-Rite in Clatchville, where I lived. I'd driven up to do a little shopping for Scott's birthday. He loved dinosaurs. He loved weapons, too, but Rudy had forbidden them. In the toy store aisle I walked past hand grenades, rocket launchers, machine guns. Then I saw a little handgun that looked absolutely authentic. I couldn't believe it was a toy. Somebody pointed that thing at me and asked for my money, you'd better believe they'd get it. That was when I remembered Danny DeVeaux. Surely he realized his gun looked real. Why would he point it at the police? Didn't he know it would mean he'd get shot? But maybe he figured they'd try to talk him out of it, like they did sometimes on police shows, or they'd just shoot him in the hand so he'd drop the gun. There were lots of episodes like that on TV, especially when the criminal was young like Danny.

It had only been a few days since the shooting. I'd found out about it when I went to the Food Lion. The News11 truck and several police cars were parked nearby. A yellow DO NOT

CROSS police line stretched around the entrance to the Bi-Rite.

There were only four registers open that day. I took Maggie's. She rang up the customers ahead of me silently, bagging their goods without meeting their eyes. Otherwise, she looked solid, as usual, with her bleached blonde hair curled tight to her head, her white tank top showing off her tan, her gold chain winking under the lights. I stepped up to the register. She nodded, her orange lips pressed together as if she were trying not to cry.

"What happened next door?" I asked.

"Supposedly some guy pulled a gun on the cops." She gave the register a hard look. "At least that's their story."

"What did the police want with him?"

"He had an outstanding warrant." She pursed her lips and leaned toward me across the counter. "Somebody must have reported him. Somebody in the store. Whoever it was, they were the ones that did him in."

"Who would do that?" I asked Rudy later that same night. We'd just seen the eleven o'clock news—11 on 11, as they called it—which repeated the story. The camera zoomed in on the toy gun.

"Do what?" Rudy asked.

"Who would report him?"

Rudy looked blank.

"You know the dead guy was black."

Rudy was sitting on the couch, elbows on knees, chin in hands. The light from the TV winked from his round glasses. He looked more like a rabbi than a Presbyterian minister with his curly dark beard that rested on his big barrel chest. But so far, in Clatchville, this hadn't given him any trouble.

He got up from the couch and bent over the armchair where I was sitting. He kissed me on the lips, the frames of our glasses scraping. "Why would you torture yourself over this?"

"It happened so close by."

"A guy I know is a criminal pulls out a gun and points it at me, I'm going to try to shoot him first. I've never shot anyone before, I'm probably going to go a little nuts. I'm probably going to keep pulling the trigger."

"Ten times?" I asked.

He shrugged, then yanked on my arm. "Come to bed."

But my mind was spinning. I went to the cabinet and got out the bourbon. I poured myself a glass.

"All right then." Rudy didn't sound happy. He went up the stairs.

After awhile, the bourbon slowed me down. I sat in the arm-chair with the TV picture on, but pushed the mute button on the remote. For awhile I just stared at the screen thinking of Maggie-the-cashier doing the same, her ratty little terrier in her lap, cigarette smoke encircling her head. What kind of night was it for Maggie or worse, for Paula, the Bi-Rite pharmacist? Had Paula seen Danny get blown away? What about Debbie, the slow-witted cashier with the beehive hairdo who always gave Scott a treat? After the last robbery at the Bi-Rite, she'd told me she wasn't taking any more shit—then, knowing I was the minister's wife, blushed and said, "Excuse my French." Had she been the one to recognize Danny, remember his outstanding warrant and call the police? What was she, some kind of racist?

* * *

At the toy store in Wheatley I stood looking at the gun. I stood there in the toy aisle, amazed. I badly wanted a shot of whiskey from the flask in my purse, but a fat woman down the aisle was handing her son a rifle.

I carried the gun and a package of dinosaurs to the check-out counter. I bought the thing. I wanted Rudy to see it. I wanted him to show it around the church and ask people in his congregation what they thought.

Don't ask me why. I hadn't been to church in a month. Did I believe in God? No. Did I want to support Rudy? Sometimes. The week before, when I'd said I felt sick and couldn't go to church with him, he wasn't too happy. In the bedroom, he flung his towel over his shoulder and went to the ironing board. He worked over his white shirt, his back to me. I could tell by the way his shoulders hunched that he was nervous. I knew what he wanted. He wanted me to come to church, hear his sermon, and afterwards, reassure him. He'd say, "How was I?" I used to say, "You were perfect, wonderful, best you've ever been," but lately all I could say was "Fine." When I said "Fine" I knew what would happen. He'd get quiet for awhile, sucking his lips, until I put dinner on the table. After awhile I'd say something like, "How's dinner?" and he'd say, "Fine" in a mean, flat voice. Scott would look down at his plate and say, "It's good, Mom," but then he'd stop eating.

Later that night Rudy would put his hands on me and say, "How are these breasts? Fine." Or, sliding his fingers under my panties, "How's that ass? Fine."

Finally I'd give up. "You were perfect today, honey," I'd say. "Best you've ever been." Then he would kiss me and I would let him because what choice did I have? and so on.

Had there ever been sermons I liked? Back when Rudy still remembered what it was like to be stuffed into a trash can by the kids on his street and rolled down a flight of stairs, yes. But lately Rudy was comfortable. Lately he just, as they say, got into the sound of his own voice. When he did, he often asked rhetorical questions such as, "Do we really want the rest of our lives to be empty?" I wanted to shout, "Sure!" So I thought it best I just stayed home.

"I'd like to come and hear your sermon," I said to Rudy, "but

I feel miserable. I'm afraid I'd sneeze in the middle and have to leave."

Rudy cleared his throat, let the iron steam, and pressed it onto his collar. "I'll just do what I did last week and the week before that. Take Scott to Sunday School, make excuses for you. Of course one of these days people are going to wonder. They're going to think you don't like them or you don't like me. When they do, what do you want me to tell them?"

I didn't see why I had to answer that.

"I asked you a question," Rudy said.

"Tell them I'm sick," I said.

Rudy looked at me angrily. "Are you, Sally?"

I sneezed. "What do you think?"

"I think maybe your drinking's getting a little out of hand. I think maybe we ought to talk about that." Rudy sat down next to me on the bed.

"A little drink now and then evens me out."

"Like it did in Seattle?"

In Seattle, it was true, I had been depressed. I'd taken sleeping pills with bourbon just after the assassination attempt on Reagan. Don't ask me why. I didn't vote for him. Maybe I felt guilty. The shrink said yes I did, though he didn't think it had to do with Reagan. There were probably other people I wanted to kill, but the people he mentioned—both of them my parents— were already dead.

My mother was—unlike myself—a mean drunk. If I left a toy on the floor, if I knocked over a glass, if I got my knees dirty in the playground, hung out with the wrong kid, breathed through my nose, rested my hand in my pocket, she hauled me into the kitchen, put me belly down over a chair, yanked down my pants and beat me with an electrical cord. She screamed, "I'm going to teach you a lesson you won't soon forget." Sometimes my father, the fix-it guy for the apartments, would stub out his cigarette, point a finger at me and say, "Your mother's doing you a favor."

There were scars on my ass and my back, but it was all over with.

Rudy, a social worker, paid me a visit in Seattle. He wore a long braided ponytail and had a peace sign tattooed on his forearm.

"Did you vote for Ronald Reagan?" I asked him.

"Hell no," he said. From the canvas knapsack he wore slung over one shoulder, he pulled out a Coalition for Justice brochure. Inside were details about the government selling arms to Iran and drugs on the streets to support the Contras in Nicaragua.

"Why don't they just hold a fucking bake sale?" I asked.

Rudy threw back his head and laughed.

When I got well, we held vigils against the death penalty, wrote letters to free political prisoners, chained ourselves to bulldozers, etc. Then, I don't know, after a few years, I got pregnant. Rudy got Presbyterian. We moved to the humid South.

Lately, it was true, I was drinking a little more. Scott was gone all day. Rudy had the church. What did I have?

After Rudy and Scott left for the Sunday services, I got dressed and walked down the hill to Bi-Rite. It was just one day after the shooting. Debbie-with-the-beehive was at the register talking to a policeman. She gave me a long, hard look. I walked to a far aisle, one where I figured bullets would be least likely to travel, circumnavigated the store until I came to the Benadryl aisle, picked out a package and went to the back to pay. Paula-the-pharmacist wasn't there. Instead a pale skinny girl with stringy brown hair worked the register. Her nameplate said, "Dot." A dozen red roses sat in a vase on the high counter.

I gestured toward the roses. "I'm sorry about what happened here yesterday."

The girl looked at me uncertainly. "Thank you."

"Were you here?"

She shook her head.

"It was a terrible thing."

She nodded, then held her hand out for my money. I didn't want to dally, counted out the exact change.

I turned, headed again for the far aisle, then walked quickly through the open space to the front door. Debbie, alone at the front register now, said, "What's the hurry?"

I paused. "You okay today?"

Her hair was stacked high and her round chinless face seemed to grow out of her neck. Flesh hung in soft folds from her arms. If my head had been clear, I'd have smelled her fragrance. I usually had to fight Scott to keep him from holding his nose when we got to her register. She nodded, chin disappearing.

"What happened?" I asked her.

She smiled the way people do when they don't mean to smile, but they do because they're nervous. Then they get even more nervous and smile some more, which embarrasses them again. Debbie put her fingers to her mouth, as if to stop it from smirking. She acted like she was scratching her lips. Then she gestured toward the doors, where a police car waited. "They told us not to say."

* * *

"By dog." The clerk at the Wheatley toy store counter grinned, revealing a lot of big teeth. He picked up the gun and turned it carefully. "You're not gonna use it in a hold-up, are you?"

In the car, I ripped open the packaging. I held the gun in my hand. It fit nicely. It made me feel different. I don't know how it made me feel. I slipped it under my skirt and drove home.

On the way I had to pass Bi-Rite. Everyday since the shooting, a police car had been parked in front. Up until the shooting, you understand, the Clatchville police were famous only for such things as directing traffic in front of the elementary school, getting keys out of locked cars, and writing parking tickets. Stationed in front of Bi-Rite they looked like the same police— one of them smooth-jawed and rotund, like an overweight boy in a police costume; another skinny and hook-nosed, a male version of the witch in "The Wizard of Oz." There was even a woman—blonde, petite, with a flat nose and thin lips. She was the one who'd excused me from a speeding ticket when I drove Scott to school the first day.

"Didn't you see the sign?" she'd asked, pointing in the direction I'd come from.

"Maybe," I said. "I don't know." I shook my head. "It's early. I haven't had my coffee yet."

She'd laughed—a guttural, masculine sound from such a small woman—and let me off. Since then Scott and I had always waved when we'd seen the police.

The names of the police who'd done the shooting hadn't been released. They were, the paper said, temporarily relieved of duty while the incident was under investigation. Suspended with pay. Home watching TV, out fishing, cutting the lawn . . . who knew? The newspapers had said very little, really. Nothing from the other side, which surprised me. No quotations from the DeVeaux clan—no threats of revenge from a grief-stricken brother, no photograph of the mother wailing at the funeral, no nothing.

Today's cop was boy-in-the-police-costume. He sat at the wheel, elbow out the window, cup in hand. I pulled into the parking lot and drove by slowly. I knew it was near Debbie's lunch hour. I knew her routine. My blue Toyota reflected perfectly in the glass of the front window. I could see everything, even the dent in the fender where I'd run the car into a tree. But I couldn't see Debbie.

I cruised out of the parking lot back onto the main road, then turned off onto Salt Street. It dead-ended into Hopewell which led, eventually, to my street. I parked at the top of the hill and walked past the houses. I didn't know which was the DeVeaux's. A black toddler rode his Power Wheels on the sidewalk, a young woman walking behind. I looked at her, but she didn't smile. Laundry hung on someone's line, not drying fast, since there was no breeze. True, at the bottom of the street, there was a warehouse with a weedy parking lot, but that was about the worst thing.

From the junction of Salt and Hopewell I drove past townhouses, a swimming pool, then further up the mountain to the nicer homes with the expansive lawns, like ours. Or should I say, Valley Presbyterian's. It was close to two o'clock. School would let out soon. I poured some whiskey into a glass. The phone was ringing, but I let the whiskey slide down my throat. The answering machine picked up. Scott was in trouble. Could I come to the office now? They'd been trying to get me all morning.

* * *

Scott's eyes were red and swollen, his little shoulders hunched up. He was only six, you remember. I said, "Oh, honey," and he said, "I'm tired."

Scott looked a lot like Rudy, but he was built like me. Skinny. And for his age, small, smaller than average, small enough that every year, when we went for his physical, we studied his growth chart anxiously.

"I was just playing," Scott said. "I didn't mean it."

"What did you do?"

"We were playing police." He looked off to the side and shrugged. "I was just playing," he said again. Then his face collapsed and he hugged me tight, like when he was a toddler and didn't want to sleep alone and I was telling him he had to and he was begging me to stay because there were monsters, couldn't I see them?, and only I could keep them away.

Dr. Williams, the principal, wore a gray skirt, jacket and heels. She'd cut her hair short, like a drill sergeant's, though her features made her look Barbie-esque.

"Scott was pretending to shoot people in the playground. He sat on Derek and wouldn't let him up, even when Mrs. Wallace asked. He knows we don't play that way here. If we do, we are sent home. This way we learn."

She bent down to Scott's level. "Scott," she said. "You may come back tomorrow if you promise not to behave that way again."

She was so close I could see the line of make-up where it started just below her chin.

"You see how small he is, Marge," I said to Dr. Williams, who stood up when I used her first name. "How could he have been sitting on someone?" I imagined flicking my fingers at her head, watching it pop off at the make-up seam.

* * *

On the way home I bought my son an ice cream cone. I told him his dad didn't have to know what happened at school. I said I knew how it felt to be the smallest kid in the class. It made you mad sometimes. It made you want to do things.

"I wish I'd sat on some people when I was your age," I told my son. "Not just kids either."

I went ahead and gave him his new dinosaurs early. I could

get him something else for the birthday. We set up the figures on the coffee table. Scott attacked my little Gallimimus, and I made terrible gasping sounds until he giggled.

By the time Rudy got home, I was dying for a drink. Rudy came in whistling, put Scott on his shoulders and did a little dance. "Daddy wrote a fantastic sermon today. Daddy is a genius." Rudy no longer had a ponytail. Using a very painful and expensive method, he'd had his tattoo removed.

I started tearing up lettuce into a salad bowl, tearing it up savagely.

"Oh," I said.

"What?"

"I forgot to get cooking oil."

Rudy circled the room, bouncing around with Scott. "So?"

"We have to have cooking oil for the chicken." I put the salad bowl aside. "I'll just run to the store real quick."

I drove down the street, up a hill and into a woods I know. Pulled over. Drank some whiskey. Oh, it was good. Then drank some more. Then I wanted a cigarette. I don't smoke, normally, but a cigarette was all I wanted.

I drove past the shopping center, turned around, then drove past again; turned around again and headed out to the Interstate. Forgetting the cigarettes, I pushed the pedal to the floor, climbing the mountains, then let off, coasting down the hills. The hills were like water, like big waves. I imagined one breaking over the car. Now and then, I sipped from my flask. I kept the windows rolled down. Finally—I can't say why—I got off at Simpsonville, turned around, and headed back. It was 5:30 p.m. I don't know that I had formulated a plan. But it didn't surprise me to find myself waiting for Debbie. It didn't seem strange to me at all that I knew exactly when she got off and which way she headed from Bi-Rite.

She walked along the sidewalk with one shoulder drooping

under the weight of her pocketbook.

I slowed the car to match her pace. "Debbie," I called. "It's me." I took off my glasses. "Scott's mother. Would you like a ride?"

Debbie's mouth hung open in surprise, then widened in a slow, stupid smile. "Well. Well, that's really nice of you." She pointed down the street. "But I'm really not going too far. My house is just up there."

"That's all right," I said. "I'm going that way. You might as well have a ride."

I stopped the car and held the door open for her. She got in with a submissive expression, like an obedient child. "It's just over the rise," she said, pointing again.

"I know."

"You do?"

I smiled, hoping I looked benign. "You just told me," I reminded her.

"Oh yeah." She giggled. "Silly me."

Her fragrance filled the car with an oppressive sweetness. I held my head half out the window, trying not to gag. I drove the car slowly up her street. She lived in a duplex next to a gas station. The duplex was painted yellow, its lawn knee high. A cat lay, ears flattened, on the driveway. It swished its tail and ran when the car pulled up.

"Oh, Mittens," Debbie called in a high voice. She started to get out the door.

"Wait," I said.

She looked back at me.

"I want to ask you something."

"Sure," Debbie said. She closed the door. "I really appreciate the ride. It's been a long day." She ran the back of her hand across her forehead. "Whew."

"Look, I know you're not supposed to talk about the shooting."

"That's right." Debbie nodded her head emphatically.

"But I don't want to ask you about that. I just want to know something about Danny DeVeaux. Was he nice?"

She nodded.

"Did you ever think he'd be shot?"

She shrugged.

"Why would anybody want him arrested?"

"Well," she said, blowing her cheeks out. "Well, he did rob people."

"Why?"

"They say it was drugs."

"So he wasn't nice."

"No," she said. She held a hand to her forehead. "Yes." She shrugged. "No and yes."

"But he pulled out that toy gun."

"I didn't know it was a toy," she said. "I was scared. But we're not supposed to talk about it." She began to get out the door, but I grabbed her arm. I held her there.

"I need to know what happened, Debbie," I said. "I won't tell anyone you told me. I can keep a secret. My husband's a minister, you know. I think you need to tell somebody. I think it'll make you feel better. Kind of like a confession. You're not Catholic, are you?"

Debbie shook her head. "Oh my no." She pulled her arm away from me, then straightened out her uniform. She looked at her house, then out at the street through the front windshield. "Are you going to let me go?"

"Try to understand," I whispered. I don't know why. I guess it was to be dramatic. Whatever worked.

She didn't move.

I reached across her lap and opened the door. "I'm not going to force you. If you tell me you'll tell me because that's what you need to do."

She slid her legs out the door.

"Who called the police?" I asked.

Debbie's lips pinched in like a parrot's beak. "Who called the police?" she asked in a mimicking voice. "That's what all of them want to know. You want to know who called the police? Somebody that didn't want to be robbed no more."

She started to get out of the car, but I grabbed her arm again, pulled the toy gun from beneath my skirt and held it up to her temple, like I'd seen in the movies.

She started to scream, then stopped herself, as if I'd instructed her to be quiet.

"Go ahead and scream," I said. "You've been quiet long enough." I poked the gun into her temple. I didn't hurt her. I just poked it gently, but it produced the desired effect. She screamed, all right. A man from the duplex next to hers came out onto the front porch in his shorts and a white T-shirt.

"She's got a fucking gun to my head," Debbie screeched.

The man shaded his eyes like a mariner searching the horizon for shore, then backed toward the door and disappeared into his house.

Now Debbie's forehead glistened with perspiration. She was really sweating. Sweating like a stuck pig. I have to say this made me feel good, because after all she was alive and Danny wasn't. It seemed like justice. I burned all over. If the police came, I might point my gun at them, too. I held the pistol steady. I was enjoying myself.

"So how's it feel?" I asked Debbie, poking the gun hard enough into her temple this time to make her cry. "How's it feel, big girl?"

TRAILER PEOPLE

It was warm enough, at 10 a.m., that people were already water skiing on the lake. A row of pines blocked her view of the water, but Wyshona could hear the engines buzzing. She'd been sitting in her lawn chair at the campsite watching the shadows disappear, scribbling in her notebook, sipping her coffee. A bear had been spotted in the campground, a cute blonde ranger, maybe 20 years old, had stopped in to say.

"So watch your dog," the ranger said. "Keep him tied up. And don't leave any food out. We don't want the bear to turn into a moocher." As if to reply, Orville moaned and turned over, exposing his belly, a blonde even paler than the ranger's. "What is he, some kind of hound?"

Wyshona shrugged. "Some kind. He's a pound dog. Barely escaped death row."

The ranger straightened her ponytail. "Good for you." She glanced at the license plate on Wyshona's truck. "Virginia. Long way from home." Wyshona could see her taking stock of the tent, the backpack stove on the table. "You just like travellin' around?"

"Actually, I'm an anthropologist," Wyshona said, entertaining herself. "I'm taking notes." She indicated the pad and pencil in her lap. "Identifying the rituals and social structures of people in campgrounds." She picked up her pencil and cocked her head toward a neighboring campsite, two trailers with a tarp stretched between them, Christmas lights draped about their perimeter, their whining spaniel chained to a post. "Take those people over there," she said to the ranger, nodding toward her neighbors. She flipped through her pad, as if looking at her notes. "Wednesday night. 11 p.m. Subjects play loud music on their TV. Thursday. Midnight. Loud music again. Friday 7 p.m. Subjects throw gasoline on their fire." She looked at the ranger. "In a way you could say they're the dominant group here."

"I might be able to do something about that," said the ranger, hands on her hips.

When the ranger was out of sight, Wyshona snapped closed her pad. Actually it included a record of expenses, projected expenses, present and future income. The figures were dismal. Soon she'd have to get a job. It was late September. She'd been on the road four months. Everything cost more than she'd anticipated—not that she'd anticipated any of it at all. But it had been worth it—the leafy beauty of the Smokies with its muddy creeks, where her vowels were long; the flat cornfields of Indiana where the boy who'd replaced her lost gas cap at the service station told her he'd moved up from Florida to look after his sick grandmother and met his future wife. When Wyshona wished them good luck, he said, "Oh, I'll take good keer of her." "Take keer," she'd said for a few hundred miles as a way of saying "You're welcome" when the cashier thanked her for buying gas.

Then on to Rocky Mountain National Park, Yellowstone and the Tetons, Glacier National Park, the Columbia Icefield in Jaspar, BC, where she just about froze to death in her medium-weight bag, an event that, though she'd thought of heading for

Alaska, made her turn back south. She'd stopped—who knows why?—in McCall, Idaho, maybe because the mountains around the lake were softer, a little more like those she was used to back East, especially in the small Southwestern Virginia town she'd escaped as soon as she was able.

Yes, up to this point, her trip had been quite an odyssey, although she'd left no Penelope to keep the home fires burning, for at the moment she had no home, the home having—as they say—been broken, a word that brought to mind her former brick rancher in its Virginia Beach neighborhood cleaved in two, air conditioners still rumbling in the windows. The tall straight loblollies in the yards, the manicured azaleas, the dandelion-free lawns were supposed to keep away harm. Harm certainly wouldn't come to her when Brad was home, she'd thought. Only when he was at sea, flying over the Gulf, keeping an eye on Saddam Hussein. When Brad was gone like that, she took to praying, to whom she didn't quite know. But when he was home—perhaps this had been her sin—she did not. When he said he had to stay late at the base, she believed him. When he said he'd had a few drinks with his friends, that was all right, too. He didn't come home drunk. Drunk was her uncle passing out face-first into his plate every Thanksgiving. Drunk was her sweaty cousin pressing her up against the outhouse. Drunk was her father in the arm chair surrounded by beer cans while she or her sister changed her grandmother's diapers and got supper on the table before her mother came home from cleaning the school.

No hound dog like the ones chained behind the trailer had taught her how to sniff out deception. Where she grew up, whatever trouble there was, it hung out like the wash for everyone to see. But in the Virginia Beach neighborhood, where she had lived with Brad, a big green sign in the flower-laden entryway declared that you were in Heron's Landing, Bird Sanctuary.

Not only was there no dirty laundry—apparently no one needed clotheslines at all.

Wyshona sighed and rested her hand on Orville's head again, fondling his silky ears. He, at least, was faithful. The sun was taking over her campsite now, burning through the pines, leaving only the few feet of shade she and Orville now occupied. She threw the last of her coffee from the mug in her hand onto the ground.

"What shall we do, fella?"

Orville's tail thumped.

"Go for a walk?"

He lifted his head and wagged.

She stood up, Orville's leash in hand. "Come on. Let's see if we can find that bear."

When she stood up, Cassie—the chained-up spaniel next door—started barking, leaping in her direction, blunt tail blurred with motion, yelping and twisting in an effort to get free. She knew the dog's name because she'd heard the Christmas-light-family yell at it so often, and predictably, a man's voice called out from the trailer, "Cassie, shut the fuck up!" He opened the trailer door and lobbed a beer can at the dog. It struck her square in the snout, and she yelped even louder.

Last night there'd been a brief period when Cassie had got loose. The entire family—men, women, kids and grandparents— circled their trailers, calling sweetly. "Come on, Cassie. Here Cassie. Come get your dinner, girl."

Wyshona had wanted to yell, RUN CASSIE RUN. Why would the dog want to return to her chain and her abuse? Every day Cassie whined and paced in the circle around her post. When the whining and barking got too loud, someone cursed her or threw something at her or backhanded her across the snout. RUN CASSIE RUN, Wyshona thought. NEVER COME BACK. She imagined Cassie, snout to the ground, ears flopping merrily, tail going like a propeller, roaming the woods, some pleasant person in L.L. Bean clothes who didn't own a television and who supported public radio finding her and taking her in. She imagined the newly adopted Cassie on one of those cushy dog beds in front of a woodstove, her coat brushed to a shine.

But the stupid dog had come back. She wagged at her abusers as if they were friends. They chained her up again, lowered themselves into their lawn chairs, and turned on their television. Loud.

"Ah hate stupid peahple," bellowed the TV comedian Jeff Foxworthy in his country-western voice, and Wyshona thought, Then you hate yourself.

If she could have kicked in their TV set, unstrung their Christmas lights, and pushed their trailers into the lake, she would have done it. They would only populate the world with cowering dogs and miserable children. They'd leave beer cans strewn along the lakes and rivers, and the butts of their cigarettes would litter the beaches, common as their belches and farts.

Cassie's barking and yelping was coming, now, from inside Wyshona's head. Each yelp carried a ping that penetrated her right temple. Her eyes ached. She clenched her jaw, locked her truck and walked along the paved loop of the campground, heading for a trail she'd seen earlier. Orville kept the leash taut, as usual, nose to ground. Trailers occupied their pull-throughs, hoses and electrical cords extended to the hook-up posts—alien rectangular creatures feeding through some bizarre umbilicus. She should have gone backpacking. It was a mistake to let herself be rounded up into this zoo. Such zoos should be outlawed, the primitive creatures they attracted stuck into a suburb someplace and shot. She despised the RVs, especially those with Christmas lights, TV antennae, generators and air conditioners riding their tops. Why go camping? Why not stay home? Orville yanked at the leash, pulling her arm from the shoulder. It was getting hot. She swatted at a black fly that stung the back of her leg.

What was it the Taoist said? Do you want to improve the world? Absolutely, Wyshona thought. Let's start by getting rid of all the RVs and those who inhabit them. The noise, the clutter, the litter. All that is obnoxious. Those who deceive us and those who let us down. Let's blot out hurt and sorrow, hunger and sickness. Adultery, divorce, enforced isolation. But the Taoist answered his own question: I don't think it can be done.

Miraculously, Cassie finally stopped barking. For a few moments, the campground was still, most of the occupants flee-ing the heat, heading for the lake with their life preservers and inner tubes. She could hear more boat engines revving. Those too, she thought. Let's get rid of those too.

A few children ran by, chasing each other, making her chest ache. By now, back in Virginia Beach, she'd be a month into her third-grade class. They'd be learning their cursive, always a particular delight, like teaching them a secret code. This would be the first time in five years she didn't have her own class. Possibly she'd thrown the proverbial baby out with the bath water, but she'd wanted nothing to remind her of her former life, not even the predictable and soothing rhythms of the school year.

A little girl on a pink and purple bike pedaled past, her freckled face solemn under a baseball cap. Wyshona recognized her by the round glasses and brown pigtails. She belonged to the Christmas lights. The family, an odd assortment—as she'd gath-ered from overhearing their loud conversations—consisted of parents, grandparents, and a couple of hulking uncles as well as three boys who already spit tobacco juice and a baby who, judg-ing by the wailing, must have had colic. Wyshona had been camping in her spot for four days, and for those four days she'd watched the girl play quietly by herself, pedaling her bike around the circle. Occasionally they took the girl to the lake, but more often than not, her mother was left tending the baby while her father, the uncles and the boys went out in the speed boat. Wyshona guessed the girl might be eight or nine—close to the ages of Wyshona's third-graders.

When Wyshona got to the trailhead, the girl was already there, straddling her bike, studying the sign. A pink lunch basket was strapped to the handlebars of her bike. She looked at Wyshona. "Are you going on this trail?"

Wyshona nodded.

"Does your dog bite?"

Orville was already wagging his tail, jaws open in a grin. "No. You can pet him."

The girl reached out a hand. "I have a dog, too."

"I know. Cassie."

The girl looked at Wyshona with surprise. Orville rubbed his snout into the girl's hand. She giggled. "His nose is wet."

"What's your name?" Wyshona asked.

"Rose."

"Nice name. I'm Wyshona."

"Oh." She put the kickstand down to park her bike. She put her arms around Orville.

"I think he likes you," Wyshona said.

Orville licked Rose's face.

Rose looked up at Wyshona. "Where are your kids?"

"I don't have any."

"Oh." Rose put her face in Orville's fur, then rested her cheek on his back. "Does that make you sad?"

"A little." She and Brad had been putting off the decision. Good thing, she supposed—though who knew? A baby might have convinced him to stay home nights.

"My mom says she'd be sad if she didn't have us."

Wyshona had noted the mother's washed-out face and flabby arms, the desperation with which she smoked cigarettes when the baby was sleeping. There was a grandmother, too, a large woman with several chins who sometimes jiggled the baby, singing it songs, but more often than not sat in her trailer, watching television.

"If you're going on this trail, can I come with you?" Rose asked.

"Would it be okay with your mom?"

Rose puckered her face. "She won't even notice."

Wyshona winced. "But if she did, would it be all right?"

Rose pointed to her lunch basket. "Well she did pack me a lunch. She said I should go off and play and eat my lunch someplace."

Wyshona shrugged. "All right. Okay. Why not. Orville and I would be glad for your company."

The trail, wide and graveled, practically a road, was marked for mountain bikes, but just now no one else was in sight. Rose pedaled ahead, making Orville whine and strain at the leash, yanking Wyshona's arm as she struggled to hold him back.

Finally Rose stopped her bike. "You know." She blinked her eyes at Wyshona. "Nobody's on this trail. You could probably just let him go."

"He would love a good run," Wyshona said. "And he does pretty well at coming when I call. As long as you're not scared of him." Rose shook her head. Wyshona thought briefly about the ranger's warning, the bear, but it was late morning. No doubt the bear was holed up someplace in the shade. Even if it were still nearby, black bears were rarely aggressive. Wyshona unclipped the leash from Orville's collar. "Okay, boy."

Orville sprang away joyously, galloping next to Rose's bike, and for a moment it was as if Rose were Wyshona's own little girl, riding along next to the family dog. They were all in a

Disney movie, weren't they?—and Wyshona was—healthy white woman, though with kinky hair and crooked teeth—the perfect Disney mom. Oh, if only all really was right with the world, if only everything and everyone were in place like that, Disney mom with father off felling a tree but sure to be home by the fireside that night, loyal as Old Yeller.

The sky was so blue it was almost purple above the pines. Huckleberry bushes grew densely in the understory. Occasionally Wyshona plucked one off its twig and popped it into her mouth, savoring its tart flavor. She paused to read a sign about how the ponderosa pine forest was maintained by controlled burning. The controlled burns were also responsible for the pleasant openness under the trees. Very different from the tangle of the eastern forests. Controlled burn. Wyshona liked the idea. Metaphorically speaking, it suggested a kind of passion she could live with. Monogamy, for instance. She sighed and craned her neck backward to look at the sky, trying to clear her mind of the oft-recurring image she had of Brad screwing some other woman.

"It is cool under the pines," she said aloud. It was a habit that averted hysteria, narrating the present to herself. The sun was intense, though, where it burned through the forest. "You're going to be all right." She'd had many moments of peace by herself next to her campfires. However, she reminded herself, at the moment she was not on her own. At the moment she was Disney mom. Orville and Rose had disappeared from view, and gradually she became aware of noises ahead, something like screaming and growling.

"Oh shit." She launched into a dead run along the graveled path, forest blurring on either side of her, feet occasionally slipping on the rocks, lungs aching, calf muscles straining, not sacrificing speed but pushing, pushing, until she could see something ahead. First she made out Rose and the bicycle, Rose standing and clutching the handlebars, Rose screaming and crying as she looked off into the woods where Orville was apparently fighting with some kind of big dog—a black Lab?—no, not a dog at all; it was a bear, a small bear but bear enough to do some damage. Orville was bleeding—she could see that as she closed up the distance between them, just as she could see that he was nevertheless holding his ground, keeping himself between Rose and the bear although he could have got away quite easily; he was clever and fast in the woods. He kept leaping for the bear's throat, but the bear, although small, was still bigger than Orville, and with a swat of its paw the bear sent Orville yelping back.

"Orville!" Wyshona got up next to Rose, squeezed the girl's shoulder, then grabbed a big stick she saw lying on the ground next to a deadfall and advanced on the bear. "Get away, you! You fucking brute. Get off my dog!" She waved the stick. She wanted to kill the bear, wanted to bash its stupid skull in. "Orville, come!"

But Orville kept leaping after the bear which, seeing Wyshona, had become distracted, so that Orville was able to clomp his jaws into the bear's chest. The bear bellowed and bit Orville's neck. Wyshona heard a pop like the breaking of a stick. The dog fell in a heap, whimpering, and Wyshona rushed at the bear, waving the stick. The bear turned and ran.

Wyshona knelt over Orville. His head had fallen at an odd angle. She stroked his ear, then put one hand under his head, lifting it slightly. His big jowls rested on her hand. Saliva dripped from his mouth, wetting her fingers. The ground was dry and hard, and the dust coated his fur, turning it brown except where the bear had bitten and scratched him, opening big, ugly wounds on his neck and back. He had been barking and leaping only a moment ago, ignoring her calls as he bit into the bear's chest. Now he was still, his eyes shut. A clump of the bear's black fur was still stuck to his nose. If she had not called him, if she had not interfered, perhaps he would have kept his distance from the bear. Perhaps he would be limping along with her now, as she took him back along the trail to the campground, Rose walking her bike beside them.

"Rose?"

Wyshona looked back at the path, but the girl and her bike were gone. Just as well. Let her go back to the campground, Maybe get some help. The bear had turned and run in a direction opposite the bike trail. Rose would be all right.

She gathered Orville into her arms. Usually when she tried to hold him, he bore the weight of his own head, sometimes waving his paws in the air as if he were swimming. The memory made her cry. She lifted Orville and started to carry him along the path. His blood smeared on her hands, her T-shirt. She staggered under the weight of his body, as she had staggered into the truck under the weight of her gear after Brad had told her he didn't want to cheat on her anymore, he was in love with someone else. Orville had been standing next to Brad on the porch. When she'd called him, he bounded into the passenger seat gleefully, hoping for a walk on the beach, a good romp.

"I'm taking the dog," she'd said. Brad had watched, still wearing his khaki uniform, holding his arms folded across his belly as if he'd just been hit. That was the last she'd seen of him. Let him file the papers if he wanted a divorce. Let him try to track her down for whatever signatures he needed. Let him worry about her safety as she had worried about his for five years, especially when his ship was in the Gulf and she dreamed, again and again, of his plane going down in the water.

She could have gone home to her family but all she could think of was her grandmother, when she heard of people who'd left the mountains and got into trouble, saying, "That's what happens to them that gets above their raisin'." At least that's what she would have said back in the days when she could still talk, before that last stroke. Her sister might have understood, but with four babies of her own—pregnant at sixteen and pregnant ever since—she didn't have much left for Wyshona. Last time she'd seen them all—Easter weekend—they'd sat out on the porch admiring the new green buds on the trees and the daffodils that came up out of the earth. The men had, as usual, got drunk, the TV blared, and one of her sister's kids got stuck when he crawled under the trailer porch. The hound dogs out back howled and barked, chained to their houses until hunting season came round. They were dogs she'd pitied all her life as they paced back and forth along the length of their chains, making trenches in the dirt.

At least Orville hadn't had a life like that, though as a hound dog, he'd harbored that fatal lust for bear in his blood. She shouldn't have let him roam. Not here. Not after the ranger's warning.

He was heavy, terribly heavy. Her arms ached. Her legs quivered. Sunlight filtered through the pines, heating the woods, making her sweat. She squatted for a moment, breathing.

She wiped her eyes and looked down the path. Rose appeared, walking next to her bike, with her grandmother and a couple of her uncles, wearing their cowboy hats and bathing suits, big bellies burned red. The grandmother's floral housedress stuck to her thighs. She limped along in her sneakers.

"Oh my dear," the grandmother said, her face crumpling into her neck.

Rose looked solemnly at Orville, then at her grandmother. Her lips quivered as she touched Orville's head. "He saved me."

One of the uncles took Orville gently from Wyshona's arms. "Let me carry her for you, honey. I'll take him back to camp."

"Much obliged," Wyshona said, using an expression she'd grown up with.

The grandmother put her arm around Wyshona's shoulders. "They'll help you bury him." She smelled of cigarettes and sweat.

Leaning against her, Wyshona was a child again, resting against her mother as the bulldozer lifted her uncle's cow into its grave. "It's his own damn fault," her mother hissed as they watched her uncle standing apart from them, cap in hand, weeping. Drunk, he'd mistaken his favorite cow for a deer in the field behind his house. When Wyshona couldn't bear to look at him anymore, she gazed instead into the tangled woods and into the blue sky overhead. She closed her eyes and listened. She was glad she wasn't like the cow, stiff and dead, swallowed in that hole by the darkness and eternal quiet. It was even all right with her to listen to the growling and squealing of the bulldozer, as ugly as it was—a sound not unlike the rumbling of the RV generators as the procession passed.

PRISONER OF WAR

—for Buddy

IT WAS DIFFICULT FOR JOE YABLONSKY not to think about dying. He was 68, and a bad back had recently forced him to retire. He'd sold his bookstore to a much younger man who immediately installed a stereo system. Shoppers were now forced to listen to exotic music, whale songs, and the sound of the ocean while incense burned by the cash register. It all made Joe feel strangely displaced, as if he'd returned to the city.

The only thing that gave him any relief was walking. Standing, sitting, lying down—he was always in some degree of pain. But something about walking, whether it loosened the tight, sore muscles or forced the vertebrae into different alignments, or whether it was just because he felt more useful then, like he was going somewhere, doing something—at any rate, it worked. Sometimes, while Frannie was at work, he went for three, four walks a day, logging six to eight miles.

But it was August. Temperatures in the nineties kept him from going out as much. Forest fires burned out of control that summer, and the smoke reached the small northern Idaho town where Joe and Frannie had lived for the last thirty-six years. They were originally from Brooklyn, where Joe had been mugged in 1958, walking from the subway. The traffic that year, the summer heat and humidity and finally the mugging had made him decide to get out of the urban sprawl. Frannie hadn't been so sure. She didn't understand what they were dealing with, the sheer numbers of people who were desperate to survive. He, on the other hand, knew he'd been lucky. The muggers had simply knocked him down from behind, yanked his wallet from his pocket, and fled. It would have been easy for them to do worse—slip a knife into his back or shoot him. So when he read the ad in the New York Times about the bookstore in Idaho looking for an owner, he convinced Frannie they should take the chance.

They arrived when the wheat was green, fertile fields rising and falling like the breasts of a sleeper, sheltering the clean town. They'd thought they might raise a family—in fact, the safety of their future children was the argument that finally persuaded Frannie, but she was unable to conceive, so they lived quietly, happy enough with the rhythms of ploughing and planting, harvest and the burning of the stubble that surrounded them. Lately field burning was banned because of drought conditions and high winds. Joe sat indoors with air conditioner going, reading everything that came in the mail, even the sweepstakes entries. He wrote letters to people who hadn't heard from him in years. He listened to the radio, his back stiffening.

Finally one afternoon he got the idea of walking up Shoulder Mountain, under the cool shade of the pines. It was the highest in a small range of green humps rising above the undulating fields of wheat and lentils and rapeseed on the Palouse prairie. He'd been meaning to hike to the top for years, but instead he and Frannie had used their time off to go to the cities—

Spokane, Seattle, or Portland—driving the varicolored Pontiacs they'd had over the years. Now, though, even in the Western cities there were increasing reports of violence—the same gang wars and racial tensions he was accustomed to hearing about in the East. But he and Frannie knew how to avoid the bad sections of the cities. And they knew they'd be returning to their safe haven in Idaho.

He pushed himself out of the chair where he'd been reading. The day was already hot, but the smoke had cleared. He imagined himself sipping cool water from his thermos under the pines, seeing the Palouse, checkered by farmers' ploughs, spread before him like a tablecloth.

He drove the Pontiac out of town onto the gravel roads. Small patches of trees appeared at the edges of wheat fields. He admired the neat houses perched at the tops of hills, horses grazing in their pastures. He and Frannie had thought of moving out of town when she retired, waking to the songs of meadowlarks instead of the coarse chirps of starlings. When they were younger the two of them had once spent a week in an isolated cabin by a lake. There was no phone. Oddly enough, even though Joe'd been mugged in a place where, theoretically, help was available, he'd felt more vulnerable than ever before in that cabin. It was the only time in his life he'd wanted a gun.

The road turned to dirt and steepened, but Joe kept the Pontiac on course. Finally he parked on a wide shoulder. He walked up the road at a leisurely pace, looking off to the sides. Sunlight filtered through the firs, stippling the ground. Now and then, squirrels chattered, scampering across fallen logs. A grouse blasted up from the brush beside him, and he shouted, frightened by the explosion of wings, then laughed at himself. His laughter sounded good in the forest. He put his hands in his pockets and peered into the dense vegetation more carefully as he walked. Several flickers sailed between dead trees in one clearing, and high in the pines he could hear the calls of smaller birds.

He'd just topped a hill and stood breathing heavily, admiring the view—golden hills undulating into the blue-rimmed horizon—when he heard engines. Soon he could see dust rising below, spiraling upwards as the vehicles traversed the mountain road, and he cursed. He moved off the road into the woods. As the cars passed he could see that they were full of young men with close-cropped haircuts. They looked at Joe as they passed, some raising their hands in greeting. Joe nodded, but kept his hands over his nose and mouth to keep from breathing the dust. After awhile, he could hear the engines die, then voices and car doors slamming.

He walked on, curious. Dust still hung in the air. Around the next curve he could see the cars. Young men milled about, laughing and shouting as if they were at a party, all of them carrying rifles and dressed in fatigues. As Joe approached, a stocky, dark-haired man who looked a little older than the others and was dressed in civilian clothes walked out from the crowd to greet him.

"What are you, ROTC?" Joe asked.

The man nodded. He was healthy and powerful, with a good, strong-looking back. He wore a T-shirt splattered with paint spots, but beneath them the word "Judge" was printed.

"Wargames?" Joe asked.

The man nodded. "One team gets a head start to organize an ambush. Then my men walk down the road, trying to anticipate."

"What do they shoot, blanks?"

"Paint pellets," said the man, pointing to the spots on his T-shirt. "The goggles are to protect their eyes." He pointed to a cluster of men whose goggles hung around their necks.

"What about you?"

"I'm the judge." He pointed to the lettering on his T-shirt. "I walk in the back. Usually I don't get shot, but someone got funny."

"Would it be safe for me to walk on up?" Joe nodded past the congregated men.

"Sure." The judge grinned. "We don't shoot civilians."

Joe made his way through the crowd. The men parted respectfully for him. He thought with enjoyment about how he would tell the story to Frannie. In a way he wanted to stop and watch, maybe walk with the judge. But in another way he wanted to get on up the mountain before all the young men did. He began to move faster, as if he were racing them.

Soon he could no longer hear their shouts and laughter, and though dust coated the brush beside the road, the air itself was cool and refreshing. He took a deep breath and congratulated himself for gaining distance on the young men so quickly. Maybe he hadn't lost a certain athletic spirit after all. He'd heard of men just a little younger than himself winning marathons. His back couldn't take the punishment of jogging, but there might be some other way to make his mark. He saw himself in the winner's circle, his legs firm and muscular, head bowed to receive a medallion. Frannie stood to one side, pride bringing the blood to her cheeks so that her skin was pink and beautiful.

When he heard the report of a gun, he stopped. There was a crashing in the brush, and he yelled, "Civilian! I'm a civilian!" A deer leaped into the road in front of him, a blue paint spot over its heart, panting, wild-eyed, and was gone. He heard men's voices and laughter.

"Come out of there!" Joe yelled. "Goddamnit, come on out!"

Two young men dressed in camouflage emerged from the woods, their faces painted black. They pointed their guns at Joe, but he stood stubbornly with his arms to his sides. "You're not here to scare the wildlife."

"We're taking you hostage, sir," the shorter man said apologetically.

The other man, taller, and with a broad face that might have looked innocent had it not been blackened for the game, spat tobacco juice. "Sure would hate to see that nice shirt all splattered with paint."

"Just be careful around his head, Mitchell. He doesn't have goggles."

"This is against the rules," Joe said. "Your judge told me. And what do you mean by scaring that deer? It—"

"Is he talking about Wally?" The tall one grinned. "Can you believe that fucker?" The shorter man was staring at Joe and didn't respond. "I said, can you believe him, Saunders?"

"It's got to be Wally," Saunders said without turning to Mitchell. His blue eyes looked oddly albino against the black facepaint. To Joe he said, "Wally wears that T-shirt as a joke. Once we get going, we try to play this game just like we would if there were a real war. How do we know you're not a spy? Even if you aren't, we have to ask ourselves what value you might have. We won't know that unless we take you for ransom. Maybe we could use you to get some of our POWs back."

"Like Wally," Mitchell said.

Joe sighed, but he was beginning to get interested in the game. It was certainly better than reading his junk mail. "How long will this take?" he asked, glancing at his watch.

"Wars aren't timed," Saunders said. "We try to be faithful to that."

"And if I don't cooperate?"

"I'm sorry, but we'll have to waste you."

"Waste me?"

"Boom, boom," Mitchell said, pointing his rifle at Joe's heart.

"Son of a bitch," Joe said cheerfully.

They prodded him into the woods with their rifles and walked to a clearing surrounded by dense brush.

"What now?" Joe asked.

"I'm afraid we'll have to tie you up," the shorter man said. He took some rope from his fanny pack.

"Hold on," Joe said, getting worried. "I'm an old man with back trouble. You boys skip this part and I'll sit here quietly."

"What position would be most comfortable for you, sir?"

"Did you hear me?"

"It's a goddamn jungle out there," Mitchell said. "War." He put a new wad of chew under his lips. "Can't trust nobody."

"Not even you," Saunders said to Joe. "If you hadn't trusted Wally, you wouldn't be here now."

"I didn't know the rules," Joe said.

"You've got to read between the lines, old man," Mitchell said.

"Our commander says if there's an aggressor somewhere in the world then we're all threatened," Saunders explained.

Joe thought back to his mugging. If these young men had been present, he might have a healthy spine today.

"We have to be prepared as realistically as possible for the day we meet the enemy," Saunders said.

"Do I look like your enemy?" Joe asked.

Saunders looked at him critically. "You could be."

"I thought this was a game," Joe said. "Tying me up would be real torture. You don't realize how bad my back is."

"How do you sleep?" Saunders asked.

"Flat on my back," Joe said. "On a good, firm mattress. And even then, getting up is a chore."

Saunders began to clear a section of dirt next to a fallen log. He took the butt of his rifle and scraped the dirt until it was level. "Lie down here," he said to Joe, "just like you would if you were sleeping."

Mitchell laughed.

"No," Joe said. "This has gone far enough."

Mitchell raised his rifle, but Saunders put a hand on the barrel, pushing it down. "I'm sorry about this. I really don't think we'll be more than a few minutes. It would look pretty stupid if we cut a deal to get our POWs back and couldn't make good on the trade. Even if you were here when we got back, our commander would chew us out if we didn't secure you. He wouldn't want us to trust an unknown quantity."

"A few minutes?" Joe asked. "Five or ten?"

Saunders nodded.

Joe sighed. "Well, tie me loosely." He pointed a finger at Saunders. "And don't forget. I'm doing you a favor."

He lay down on the dirt. "Got anything for a pillow?"

Saunders put down his rifle, pulled off his camouflage shirt and then the T-shirt beneath it. The sight of his pale chest embarrassed Joe, who glanced away.

"You can use this," Saunders said.

The shirt smelled of sweat, but Joe rolled it up to support his head. At least no one would say he was a bad sport.

They tied his hands and feet. Saunders was careful to ask whether the ropes chafed him and adjusted them accordingly.

"Adios, " he said, saluting before he and Mitchell disappeared into the woods.

Joe listened to the branches cracking under the boy's feet, marking the direction of their movement. Insects hummed in the still woods. He felt silly. All this to keep from being spattered with paint. Still, there was nothing funny about having a rifle pointed at his heart. The boys had played their parts convincingly.

He was grateful that he hadn't had to go to war. A touch of asthma had kept him from joining the service, but boys he'd grown up with had died, some in World War II, others in Korea, even one or two in Vietnam. A younger cousin came back whole from Vietnam, but couldn't sleep without having terrible nightmares; Joe's aunt had spoken of finding the sheets soaked through with her son's night sweats during the coldest of Pennsylvania winters. Given what Joe had missed, he supposed thirty minutes wouldn't be too great a sacrifice for the young men being trained in his country's defense. Besides, it was kind of exciting, like playing hide-and-seek as a youngster.

An insect crawled under his collar, and he lifted his tied wrists to brush it off. According to his watch, five minutes had passed. The needles of pines brushed the blue sky overhead, their cones dangling like ripe fruit. There was no wind, and the spot where Joe lay was entirely shaded except for a patch of sunlight across his legs which felt good. He closed his eyes.

In his dream, people whispered to him, but he couldn't make out the words. The people in the dream (his high school PE teacher? his father? he could barely make them out—) began to pour sand over him, lightly at first, then in bucketloads he knew would eventually smother him. The sand tickled and burned. He tried to make himself heard, forming sounds in the back of his throat.

The sounds woke him. Ants crawled along his arms and neck, tickling and occasionally biting him. He sat up and rubbed himself frantically against the fallen log. The wind had picked up, blowing smoke from the faraway fires over the sun. An hour had passed. Joe considered the knot that bound his hands. His mouth felt hot. He spotted a sharp rock some distance away, stood gingerly, feeling the pain travel up his back, and hopped over to the rock, his spine jarring with the movement. At times the pain forced him to stop and rest. Finally he knelt beside the rock and worked the rope against it until it began to fray. He sawed doggedly. The rope came loose. He chafed his wrists and untied the rope at his ankles. He felt a little sorry for the boys, but they hadn't held up their end of the bargain. Maybe they'd been captured themselves.

He started back for the road, thinking of dinner and a hot bath. His back hurt from the effort of hopping and bending over the rock. He kept to the side of the road, ducking from bush to bush so the patrols wouldn't take him. He had to crouch behind a tree when one of them went by, a group of seven moving quietly in formation. Joe's heart beat fast.

After they passed without seeing him, Joe gained more confidence. He began to walk faster. It was late afternoon. If he wasn't home when Frannie got there, she would worry. He pictured her going from room to room in their house, calling his name even though she could see the Pontiac was gone. After awhile she'd phone the police and the hospital.

It was difficult to move soundlessly in the dry woods. The crackle of dead leaves and branches made Joe anxious. Normally he walked with his spine straight, coming down heavily on his heels. Now he led with his toes and silently cursed his aching back.

Voices caused him to crouch behind a tree again, and he gritted his teeth against the burning sensation that travelled down his spine, radiating outward to his arms and upward to his neck. The voices drifted down from the direction he'd come.

"He'll be heading for his car," the voice said.

He heard a rustling sound and saw a strange soldier poking his rifle into the brush by the road.

"Yablonsky!" a familiar voice called. "Come on out! We've got your car surrounded anyway." Saunders emerged from around a curve in the road.

Joe hadn't told them his name. They must have broken into his car and read it on something in the glove box. The game, Joe decided, had gone on long enough, especially if the Pontiac was threatened. He was angry and tired. He came out from behind the tree with his hands up. "So shoot me. You said a few minutes. I waited an hour. If I don't get home soon, my wife—"

"Shut up, sir." Saunders lifted his rifle. "The war's not over."

Mitchell came around the bend and guffawed. "Shoot the bastard."

"I tell you, I'm too old for this. If you boys want to go on playing, go ahead, but don't force innocent bystanders to be part of this. Now, I've got to go home. My wife will be worried."

"The thing is, sir," Saunders said, "I can't vouch for your safety if you decide to go. Some of them have real bullets. They're not supposed to, but they do."

Joe stared at him, lowering his arms. "Young man, you have a strange sense of humor. I'm telling you, I'm sick and tired of this."

Saunders tucked the rifle under his arm and pulled a pistol from his belt. He spun the chamber, shook out a bullet and tossed it to Joe. "I'm not kidding, sir."

"Who's in charge here, anyway?" Joe shouted. "Does your commander know you boys have bullets?"

Saunders didn't answer.

"What do you think you're doing up here?" Joe asked. "What do you think you're fighting for? Aren't you supposed to make it safe for a man to walk wherever he wants?"

Mitchell laughed, and two of the soldiers Joe didn't know shifted toward one another, smiling.

"We're just playing, sir," Saunders said. "But we take winning pretty seriously."

"Your commander's going to take it seriously when he hears what you've been up to."

"You're making it imperative that we keep you here."

"We could turn him into coyote bait," Mitchell said.

Joe appealed to the other two soldiers who stood off to the side, watching. "Don't you boys know how much trouble you could get into? Threatening a civilian with paint pellets is bad enough, but real ammunition could land you in jail. Being ROTC doesn't excuse you from the law."

"Who told you we were ROTC?" Saunders asked.

Joe looked at them more closely. He'd thought they were all college age, eighteen or so, but maybe it was just the uniform.

"If you're not ROTC, what are you?"

"We're just boys, sir. Preparing ourselves for war."

"What war?"

"There's always war."

Beneath the black paint, Saunders face was fresh and earnest. He could be any local farmer's son.

"Where'd you get your weapons?"

"I can't tell you that."

Joe imagined grain silos full of automatic rifles and explosives. He'd heard of a used car salesman in Idaho Falls who'd bought scraps from a nuclear facility—scraps enough, it turned out, to build several atomic bombs. Frannie'd been very upset. What if the so-called scraps had fallen into the wrong hands? She said they ought to write letters of protest to their senator, let him know how they felt about what the government called its "indiscretion," but Joe didn't see how it would help.

"We can't let the son of a bitch go now," Mitchell said. He moved toward Joe threateningly.

Joe still found himself unable to believe the boys weren't play-acting. He was only a few miles from his home. Frannie was wrapping things up at the lawyer's office. Toys were strewn across front lawns, and soon, parents would sit exhausted in front of their televisions. As the sun sank, sprinklers would come on in Joe's neighborhood.

"I'm going home now," Joe said. He turned his back on the soldiers and began to walk down the hill.

"Yablonsky," Saunders said. "That's Jewish isn't it?"

"Polish," Joe offered over his shoulder. He felt a warning chill prickling his scalp and stopped. "Who the hell are you?"

Saunders smiled.

"Who's your commander?"

Saunders shook his head. "Go on." He nodded down the hill. "You won't get far."

"What's the fucking hold-up?" Mitchell asked. "Why not get him now?"

Saunders turned to Mitchell. "I say let him go on home. What's he going to do? Call the cops? They'd think it was all an old man's nightmare. Isn't that right, Yablonsky? What would you think?"

"Fucking bastard," Mitchell said . "He wouldn't think nothing as long as his own ass was comfy-cozy."

"You know where he lives," Saunders said to Mitchell. "And now he knows you know, and he knows if he talks about us, we'll be coming after him."

"Slimy, motherfucking Pollack," Mitchell said. He fired a paint pellet at the ground in front of Joe. Joe backed away slowly, then turned and ran.

"You're dead, Yablonsky!" Mitchell yelled.

A contingent of men came at him up the hill. Joe's chest burned. He dropped to his knees, panting. When the soldiers took him by the arms he looked into their faces. He'd seen all of them before, in the photographs of uniformed young men on the pianos and buffets of his retired friends, in the old movies of boys marching happily toward war. They were faces full of power and certainty, the excitement of conquest, faces which probably folded in on themselves from boredom when they got home.

In the distance, he heard a shot, and it made him think of the volley fired over his veteran cousin's grave, the only other close, live gunfire he'd ever heard. The mournful sound of

"Taps" and the regular, inevitable rhythm of the soldiers marching in formation away from the grave had moved him profoundly. But now the way the boys operated together, dragging him back up the hill toward Saunders, swarming through the woods, made him think of millions of tiny spiders bursting from their eggs, nests of rattlers awakening in their pits, maggots burrowing blindly into carcasses.

The soldiers brought him up to face Saunders. Joe breathed deeply, trying to calm down. "All right. You boys have just got carried away. I'll go home and forget all about it. Okay?"

"Take him to his car," Saunders said.

"What the hell." Mitchell grabbed Saunders' arm. "You're not going to let him go?"

Saunders didn't answer. The others obeyed him. Joe walked between the two soldiers who held his arms.

"I don't have to listen to you," Mitchell said to Saunders. The boys were behind Joe now, but he heard the sound of scuffling, a few low thuds, and a moan. The soldiers kept Joe moving. Before long he saw his car. One door stood open. Otherwise it looked all right. They must have jimmied the door open gently. With relief, he noticed that the interior light was on. The battery was probably still okay. In a few seconds he'd be driving down the road toward home. He longed to reach into his pocket to feel his keys—in a sudden panic he was afraid they might have fallen out of his pocket when he was tied up—but the soldiers still had a tight hold on each of his arms.

They stopped in front of the car and turned slightly to look behind them, awaiting further instructions. Saunders stood a few yards back and up the hill with his legs apart. There was no sign of Mitchell.

"You won't regret this," Joe said.

"I know," Saunders answered.

"I won't say anything to anyone."

"No, I expect you won't."

The soldiers still held onto Joe's arms. "They can let go now. I won't even tell my wife."

Saunders nodded at the soldiers, and they released Joe, who stood feeling dazed for a moment, rubbing his arms, then dug in his pocket and closed his fingers gratefully around his keys. He got into the car and started the engine. The soldiers moved out of the road as he turned the car around. He couldn't believe his luck. They must be ROTC after all, and afraid he might get them into trouble. They must have been playing with him all along.

Joe stopped the car and looked back at Saunders, who still stood on the hilltop, his legs apart. "You really had me going there for awhile."

Saunders smiled and waved.

Joe put the car in gear and coasted down the mountain, touching the brake occasionally as he headed into the curves. He felt oddly elated. Though the car bumped over ruts in the road, he didn't feel the same electric jolts of pain in his back as he had on the way up. The walk must have done him good, despite the long spell on the hard ground, the soldiers' jerking on his arms, and his own dodging and running through the woods. Maybe he was in better shape than he thought. Maybe he'd make it into some winners' circle after all. Those boys were pretty good, he thought, chuckling to himself; they'd been able to do what none of the doctors, even in Seattle, thought possible, making Joe bend in ways he refused at the therapist's. He wished he could tell Frannie about it, but he'd made his promise. In a way he wished he could go back up the mountain another day and get in on the game. Next time he wouldn't get caught. Next time he'd ... but when he rounded the hairpin curve and started down the steep grade, there was someone next to the road—a boy who looked like Mitchell pointing a pistol at the car. Joe jerked the car away from Mitchell's side of the road. It bumped a tree trunk and sent a slide of rocks down the slope. Joe glanced in the rearview mirror and saw Mitchell still aiming the pistol. He turned the wheel and gunned the engine, moving down in his seat so his head wouldn't present a target. Something in his back caught and locked. He cried out, gripping the wheel, his teeth clamped together.

STRAY DOGS

ON OUR WAY TO THE MOVIES, carrying paper bags full of popcorn our mothers had made, May Sicchel and I were followed by an ugly yellow dog with the body of a greyhound and the head of a retriever.

"Don't pay any attention, Sherrie," May hissed when I turned to look. "Just ignore it and it'll go away."

"How do you think it got in here?" Our compound was surrounded by a high barbed wire fence, and the gate was guarded by Filipino soldiers. Every morning our fathers put on their Navy uniforms and got in their cars and drove to the Filipino base in Manila. They were gone all day. But even without them, we were safe. The bad Filipinos were outside the compound gate. So were the dogs. I saw lots of them when I rode the bus to my fifth grade class at the American School, past the shacks made of newspaper and the naked children squatting in the gutters to pee. But in the compound no one had dogs. To bring them from the States, you had to put them in quarantine.

"It probably dug under the fence," May said.

"Maybe it just wants to be petted," I said, but May answered,

"Don't you dare. It might have rabies."

Because she was often sick, May wasn't my best friend. She had bladder infections, one after another. Sometimes kidney infections. May was skinny, too, like the dog behind us, and pale. Big red freckles covered her face. But her father was a captain and mine was only a commander.

Amy, my best friend, had had to spend the day going to the commissary at Sangley Point with her mother; otherwise, I would be going to the movie with Amy. When my mother went to the commissary, I had to go along, too, though it was a long drive, and I often got carsick from the heat and the fumes of the traffic. It was easy for the Filipino driver to stop, since the traffic was going so slowly, and let me throw up. He kept a pistol on the seat beside him, in case anyone tried to hijack the car.

At the commissary Mother gave me certain aisles to search in, and like a good retriever I returned with the things she wanted. Then the Filipino workers put the groceries in bags and loaded them onto a refrigerated truck. When the truck got to our house, the maids unloaded the groceries marked with our name. But this morning my mother didn't want to go to the commissary with Mrs. Perry. Instead she had said, "Why don't you call May Sicchel? She could use a friend."

It was Mother's day to have the other Navy officers' wives over for bridge. Amy's daddy was in the Army, so her mother wasn't invited. Our Filipino maids, Sylvie and Ruth, had polished the good silver the day before, getting ready for the luncheon. I liked their rapid talk in Tagalog. Sylvie had taught me a few words, but when I said them, she just laughed at me.

Now May was taking small steps, her legs tight together.

"Dogs can smell it if you're afraid," I told her. To me the dog looked too exhausted to be much of a threat. It was falling back, losing heart, nose to the ground.

"I have to go to the bathroom," May said.

The movie theater was in a big rectangular building painted government green. We got in free. There was no place to buy candy or popcorn, which was why we had brought our own. We sat in wooden chairs with seats that flipped up, bolted in semi-circular rows in front of a curtainless screen. May and I and a few other kids I didn't know took up the middle rows. The rest of the auditorium was empty.

In the movie, Christians were either thrown to the lions or made into slaves. The heroine, a beautiful pale woman with hair the color of May's, refused to give up her faith. A Roman gladiator fell in love with her. May chewed her popcorn loudly during the most romantic scenes. I wanted to slap her, but just then the heroine was thrown to the lions. Incredibly, the gladiator rode in on his white horse and scooped her up just as a lion charged. The city was in flames.

We walked silently out of the theater. The coconut trees waved over our heads.

"If I had been her," May said, "I would've told them I didn't believe anymore. I wouldn't have let them throw me to the lions."

"Not me."

"Hey," May said, "I don't see that dog."

"Too bad," I said, in the mood to prove my courage.

We walked faster. When May got to her street, she waved quickly and turned down the block. The yellow dog came around the corner of a house. Without May, I wasn't so brave. I broke into a run, glancing back over my shoulder, but the dog had stopped to sniff at a bush.

In my own backyard, I felt safe. I picked up one of the san-tols that had fallen from our tree, opened the screen door halfway, then put the round fruit in the doorjamb. When I opened the door all the way, the fruit squished open, splitting into two perfect halves, like a ripe peach. I pulled out the large pit, popped it into my mouth and sucked it, glad for the moisture that cooled my mouth, that filled it with taste.

Through the screen door and down the hall I saw Sylvie and Ruth gliding in and out of the kitchen in their white uniforms, bare legs, and flipflops. Sylvie, a tall, thin woman who wore her long black hair in a knot at the back of her head, had once let me go into her small room behind the kitchen. From her dresser drawer she pulled out a framed picture of her nephew, Felipe. He was two years old—a dirty toddler with big dark eyes, torn shorts and no shirt who looked like the children I passed outside the gates when I rode the school bus. Sylvie said with the money she earned at our house, she could buy clothes for Felipe.

The maids' rooms, my parents had warned me, were off limits unless the maids invited me in. Ruth, walking past Sylvie's room to her own, frowned at Sylvie and me. She opened her mouth slightly, her gold tooth glittering like a fang. She said something to Sylvie in Tagalog, something that sounded angry. Sylvie shook her head and didn't answer. Ruth was older than Sylvie and thinner, with the expression of someone who—as my father put it—had just bitten into a persimmon. Her hair was short and curled wildly. I'd heard Mother say to Daddy that she didn't trust Ruth.

I spat out the seed, walked in, and stood in the doorway between the kitchen and dining room. Mother's ladies were still sitting around the table, coffee cups in front of them, eating cookies. They wore dresses cinched in at the waists that flared out into full skirts. I imagined their sandaled feet and painted toenails under the table.

"Sherrie," Mother said. "Come here, sweetie, and say hello to these ladies."

Mother smelled of gardenias. She put her cool hands on my arms and pulled me into her body. I leaned my back against her with my front to the ladies but kept my eyes on the floor.

"Sherrie's just been to see a movie," Mother said brightly.

"Was it good, honey?"

I nodded.

Mrs. O'Ganion wore a dress the color of snot. Mrs. Blake's fat pouffed out either side of her tight straps. Mrs. Holiday could barely pick up her cookie because her fingernails were about two inches long. I'd heard Mother say Mrs. Holiday's maids had to do everything, even tie her shoes, so she wouldn't break her nails. Compared to these ladies, Mother was beautiful—thin and young, with brown hair that fell to her shoulders in soft waves.

"How did you get your maids to cut those sandwiches into such pretty little shapes?" Mrs. Blake asked.

"I did them myself," Mother answered.

Mrs. Blake put a hand to her breasts, then leaned across the table toward Mother. "You shouldn't do that," she whispered. "They'll take advantage."

"Can I watch cartoons?" I whispered into Mother's ear. The TV was in the next room.

"No. We're about to play cards in there. Why not go up to your room and read?"

I went back into the kitchen, but the maids were busy. Sylvie ignored me, scraping dishes, and Ruth gave me a savage look. Eye-level with the counter, I saw a silver serving spoon, one of Mother's best, which I knew she had received as a wedding present years ago and shipped carefully from the States. It rested in a bowl of red Jello. The Jello looked good. I scooped a bite into my mouth, then clutched the spoon to my stomach and ran upstairs to my bedroom.

I put the spoon on my bed and traced the fancy patterns on the handle with my finger. Mother had told me someday I would inherit the silver. I imagined myself a beautiful lady like Mother having a dinner party. My silver gleamed. I had polished it myself. Sitting at the table admiring the settings were Sylvie and Amy Perry. Through the open window I heard the rustle of leaves and the shouts of other children. I looked outside. The Holfield kids had a hose out and were squirting each other. Our gardener stood with a rake in his hand, watching. He wore a straw hat and no shirt. Under his tattered pants, his feet were bare. I had heard Mother say he was Ruth's cousin. Mother thought he was the ugliest man she'd ever seen, small and bow-legged, like a monkey from the jungle.

The sound of the women's voices floated up the stairs and came through my closed door. They were playing cards now, and Mother was smiling her false smile. She probably had Mrs. Holiday for her partner. I imagined Mother picking up the cards so Mrs. Holiday wouldn't break her fingernails. I didn't like to think of it.

When Mother realized the spoon was missing, she'd ask me if I had seen it. Of course I'd give it back. But what if I didn't? Who would she blame?

There was a hole cut in the wall of my room that was meant as a fire escape. It was latched with a hook, and I was forbidden to play with it, because it opened onto the roof. I looked out the window again to be sure the gardener's attention was fully taken by the Holfield children, then unlatched the fire escape door and wedged the spoon between two shingles.

Heat shimmered from the black roof. Palm leaves waved overhead. The sky was clear and blue. Other two-story houses just like mine, all of them officers' quarters, rose in a neat line down the block. I couldn't see into their darkened windows, but I imagined ropes strung between the fire escapes, especially mine and Amy's, so we could climb out of our bedrooms into each other's. Below, the green lawns were neatly trimmed. I could see a gardener a couple of houses over cutting the bushes.

In California Daddy had been the gardener. He wore baggy shorts and a golf shirt. His sneakers were stained with grass.

He'd mow the lawn, then set up the sprinklers. I liked to listen to their chug-chug through the open window. One afternoon when he was finished, he washed his hands, then dried them on the towel that hung by the kitchen sink. He pushed his black-rimmed glasses up higher on his nose and ran his hand over his crewcut.

"It'll be nice not to have to do that anymore," he said. "You know we'll have a gardener at JUSMAG." JUSMAG, my parents had told me, stood for Joint United States Military Advisory Group, which was also the name of the compound where we'd be living. It sounded exciting. My parents told me the Philippines were tropical islands. Maybe there would be treasure, big chests of gold left by pirates.

Mother had been making jelly, stirring blackberries in a big pot on the stove. Her shoulders tensed. "I guess a gardener would be all right, but I don't want servants in the house."

Daddy put his hands around her waist. "I know it'll be a little weird, but we don't really have a choice. They come with the house, as I understand it. People sort of hand them down. They count on us for their living."

In California our backyard was surrounded by a redwood fence. We had a blonde cocker spaniel named Butterscotch. Beyond our fence there was a canyon. In front of the house and just beyond it, the street dead-ended, so it was safe for kids to play with their dogs running around barking. All of us rode our bikes up and down in front of the houses. No barbed wire fence, no rabid dogs or naked children, no Filipino driver who carried a gun. But on the other side of our street in the Philippines, a hill sloped down to the barbed wire fence. There were caves in the hill—old foxholes, Daddy said.

"Where are the foxes?" I had asked.

"No." Daddy laughed and pulled me up on his lap. "Foxholes are what the soldiers hide in during a war so they won't get shot."

Our side had helped the Filipinos against the Japanese before I was born. Now we were helping them some more, because, Daddy said, they were a little disorganized.

I imagined the Filipino soldiers in rumpled uniforms, unable to find their guns. Daddy and the other men from JUSMAG would help them find their weapons, or else give them some more. I knew Daddy was important to the Filipinos because he and Mother had been invited to meet their new President, a man named Marcos, who actually lived in a palace.

The foxhole near our house was full of broken glass and beer bottles. Daddy said sometimes people found helmets or old shells in there or grenades that hadn't exploded. It was dangerous, he said, and I should never go in there without an adult. Daddy said maybe there were still ghosts of soldiers in those foxholes. I knew he was just trying to scare me, but it worked. I wondered if that was where the skinny yellow dog was hiding.

I heard the front door open. It was right below me, though I couldn't see it because of the rooftop. The sound of the ladies' voices warned me to duck back into my room and latch the fire escape door.

* * *

That night, I dreamed of soldiers. Some prodded me with their rifles, making me walk down a long tunnel lit with dim lamps. Broken glass crunched under my bare feet. But my hands had long, claw-like fingernails like Mrs. Holiday's. When I turned to scratch the faces of the soldiers, their heads turned into fruit, round and ripe as santols, falling from the soldiers' bodies onto the ground.

* * *

I woke up with the feeling I'd lost something. I struggled to wake up and remember, fighting the pull of sleep. My room was gauzy with morning light, the few pictures on my walls barely visible. I stared at the one called "A Girl with a Watering Can." The girl wore a bright red bow in her hair and a pretty blue dress. She stood in a garden, looking forward, her lips curved upward and a happy expression in her eyes. In one hand she held a green watering can; in the other, two daisies. Something white, like the tail of a dog, curled behind her, as if her pet stood off to one side. The girl, I thought, was doing the job of the gardener. I wanted to be that girl. I wanted to be standing in that garden with my dog Butterscotch, picking flowers and watering plants, like I had in California. Instead I had turned into a thief. I had stolen Mother's silver spoon. Maybe Mother would blame Ruth. If that happened, we would be better off. Mother had said she didn't trust Ruth. Ruth was skinny and mean, like the stray dogs.

* * *

Mother and Daddy sat at the breakfast table drinking their coffee and reading the newspaper. Mother wore the silk robe Daddy had bought her in Hong Kong the time they left me with Sylvie for the weekend. Amy Perry's mother had checked on me, too, but mostly it was just me and Sylvie. She made my meals, told me stories and tucked me in at night. During the days, when Mother usually let me run freely on the compound, Sylvie wouldn't allow me to go out alone.

"Mother lets me," I told her, but Sylvie just smiled with her mouth closed.

She sat in the shade by the compound pool, the only fully clothed woman, crocheting as I played in the water. I kept saying, "Watch me, Sylvie," as I perfected my dives and handstands, and she looked up from her work with those almond eyes that—

even with my parents gone—never met mine.

At the table, Daddy cleared his throat and pushed his glasses further up on his nose. He brushed crumbs from the lap of his uniform. Today he wore khakis. The whites, he had explained, were only for inspections and other important occasions. When he wore them, I thought he looked like the Lone Ranger, except that on his head was a Navy cap instead of the broad-brimmed hat of the cowboy.

Mother put her newspaper down and opened her arms. I leaned against her, running my fingers along the slippery fabric that covered her arm.

"Did you have a good night?"

I nodded, though I still remembered my dream, and it made me uneasy.

Mother kissed my cheek. I sat in my chair. Sylvie brought a glass of orange juice for me from the kitchen.

"Anything else, Mum?" she asked Mother. "Mum" was the word she and Ruth used for Mother.

"Just her breakfast."

"Ruth's bringing it."

"Thank you."

Sylvie disappeared into the kitchen.

"Sweetie," Mother began as I sipped my juice, "have you seen my good silver spoon?"

"No," I said, looking carefully into my glass.

Ruth put a plate of steaming eggs in front of me without speaking, then retreated to the kitchen.

The phone rang. It was May Sicchel, wanting me to go to the pool with her. I told her I had to ask my mother, who was still at the breakfast table with Daddy, the two of them talking in low voices.

"Say no," I whispered to Mother, my hand covering the phone.

"Who is it?" Daddy asked.

"It's the Sicchel girl," Mother told him. "Sherrie thinks she doesn't like her, but she hasn't really given her a chance."

Daddy folded the newspaper carefully, then cleared his throat and pushed his glasses up on his nose. "I'm up for promotion this month. Sicchel's on the selection board."

Mother looked from him to me, then nodded. "You go with her today, sweetie. It won't kill you."

* * *

I had just changed into my bathing suit upstairs when Mother knocked on the door. She sat on the bed, pulling the belt of her robe tighter.

"Sherrie, I just want you to try to give May a chance. She can't help it that she's been sick."

"You just want me to be nice to her so Daddy'll get a promotion."

"That's not true."

I kept my back turned as if I were looking out the window, but my eyes were focused on the silver latch holding the fire escape closed.

"I want you to learn not to judge people so quickly," Mother said.

"She can't even swim," I said. "I've been to the pool with her before, you know. We have to stay in the shallow end the whole time. If I go in the deep end, she always looks like she's going to cry."

"Maybe you could help her learn. You know, while you were out learning to swim, May was sick or in the hospital."

"That's not my fault."

"No," Mother said. "It's not your fault that you're stronger than she is, either, but it is your fault if, when somebody weaker needs your help, you don't give it."

* * *

As I passed through the kitchen to go out the back door, my flipflops slapped on the floor. Sylvie turned from the sink. "Sherrie," she said, "please wait."

Ruth was wiping the refrigerator door, her movements quick and angry.

Sylvie squatted in front of me. For the first time in my memory, she looked directly into my face. "Have you seen your mother's silver serving spoon?" she asked, speaking each word carefully.

I cocked my head, thinking of a Shirley Temple movie I'd seen, trying to look as innocent as she had, my cheeks dimpling like hers.

"No," I said. "Why?"

Sylvie took a deep breath. "We can't find it. We know it was in the Jello yesterday, but today we can't find it."

"Maybe somebody stole it," I said.

"Who?" Sylvie asked, her eyes narrowing. "Who would do a thing like that?"

* * *

Heat rose from the blacktop as I walked toward the pool, and small stones caught in my flipflops, then came loose, stinging my bare legs. When I saw May waiting for me at the end of her street, the burning feeling I'd had in my stomach since breakfast got even worse. May looked like an understuffed scarecrow, her arms and legs like sticks, her stomach concave. She had freckles everywhere. We began to walk together. She was the only kid I knew whose flipflops didn't make the flipflop sound because she didn't move with enough energy.

At the pool, as I had predicted, May wanted to stay in the shallow end. Even play in the baby pool. I said no.

The pool floor sloped gradually toward the deep end. Finally I convinced May to make her way slowly toward the deeper water, going up on her tiptoes until only her nose showed above the water. She rested her hands on my shoulders, moving along like a dancer in point shoes. But then she got a little too deep. The water must have covered her nose. She grabbed me around the neck, pulling me down so I stood on my flat feet. My nose and mouth were underwater, but my eyes and the top of my head weren't. Other children swam and played around May and me, unaware that I couldn't breathe. May's grip was strong; it paralyzed me. Water splashed into my eyes from someone kicking nearby. I could hear the muffled sound of happy screams. May said nothing. She hung on. Maybe she didn't know I couldn't breathe. The edge of the pool was close, but not close enough. I reached for it, but it was just a hand's length too far. I stood in the water stupidly, thinking I never should've let her grab me. The stale air rose to my throat. If I let it go I'd open my mouth and breathe in water and drown. I grabbed May's arms, trying to push them off, but that just made her grip tighter. She was choking me. I clawed at her with my nails. Then I heard the lifeguard's whistle and saw him stand and strip off his T-shirt and jump into the water and grab May.

The lifeguard was a young Filipino man who wore his hair like Elvis Presley's and had a heart tattooed on one of his arms. He liked to talk and laugh with the American ladies. But now he wrapped May in a towel and sat her on one of the folding chairs, then extended his tattooed arm to pull me from the pool, where I clung to the side now, gasping. He wrapped a towel around me and sat me next to May. I thought he'd scold us, but he only looked frightened.

May was crying. "Why'd you take me so far out?"

There were long red scratches on her arms where I'd clawed at her, trying to get her to let go.

* * *

At home, I walked into the front door in my wet bathing suit, which was forbidden—when wet, I was supposed to use the back entrance—and tracked water across the wood floor. I went to my room and closed the door and sat, completely soaked, in front of the air conditioner. I watched the goose flesh rise on my arms and the damp spot from my bathing suit spread onto the bedspread until I was shivering so badly I couldn't stand it anymore. Then I got up and went into the bathroom and took a scalding shower.

When I came out, I heard Mother shouting into the phone.

"Can you hear me now?" she asked. The phone lines were so bad outside the compound, you had to yell to be understood. "I say I went ahead and fired her. Then Sylvie decided to go, too. They both left on the afternoon bus. We'll probably lose the gardener, too."

I paused in the hallway, listening, though I was wrapped only in a towel. Mother hesitated, then said, "Yes, I guess I'll be cooking tonight. I hope I remember how."

I got dressed and put a fresh towel over my bedspread to soak up the moisture. Then I opened the fire escape door and put my head out over the roof and thought of walking out over the shingles and leaping off. How would it feel? If I flapped my arms, would I fly? The spoon gleamed from beneath the shingles where I'd wedged it. I pulled it into my room and held it on my lap in front of the open fire escape door. When Mother knocked I didn't close the fire escape. I didn't put the spoon under my shirt or wedge it beneath my butt.

"You," she said. Her voice sounded as choked as I had felt when I used my nails to scratch May's arm. She moved into the room with quick, angry steps and yanked me up by one arm and pulled me away from the fire escape, taking the spoon with her other hand. She pushed me down on the bed and I sat staring at her bare feet, her red toenails. Her fingers dug into my shoulder, and she shook me and said, "Do you know what you've made me do?"

I said nothing.

She held the spoon by the handle and hit me with the curved bowl, spanking me with sharp, stinging slaps on my thighs while I covered my face with my hands.

"We—slap—don't—slap—steal," she kept saying. Slap, slap. "We—don't—slap slap—steal." Then she stopped and stood over me. "We don't need to steal. We aren't like them."

Afterwards she threw the spoon onto the floor. It landed with a sharp ping and then she picked it up and hurled it out the fire escape.

"Mommy," I said. I was crying.

She slammed shut the fire escape door and pushed the latch closed. "Don't you ever open this door again."

She went out of the room and left me sobbing. After awhile I calmed down and got up and looked out the window. I saw the ugly yellow dog sniffing at the ground. Maybe it had found Mother's spoon. Maybe the dog was licking the last bits of Jello. Then maybe the dog would take the spoon into its big, slobbery mouth and carry it away.

SELF-DEFENSE

I'M GLAD YOU CAME OUT HERE WITH ME. You deserve a martini. Or three. You did a great job in the workshop this week—the way you handled that old fart from Biology. Terrific. I see what you were doing. *George, I just think the way you treat your students is FABulous.* You have the tone. You have the voice. While all the time you're thinking what an asshole. You got him turned around, though. You had him eating out of your hand. Following you around like a puppy. Me, I just wanted to flatten him. Day after day around that conference table with him droning on about his students, how he'd been here for a hundred years and they'd never done it this way before. How technology doesn't equal teaching. Oh, he took the free computer all right.

Yeah, absolutely, the view up here is fantastic. The breeze isn't too much for you, is it?

Good, good, here's your martini. Here's my bourbon. Here's to us, job well done, no one killed or mutilated, everyone computer-ready, Web-oriented, blah, blah, blah. This is my third summer teaching this stuff. Of course it's new software every year, new stuff to learn. But the resistance is the same. Every year somebody like the old man from Biology.

If I'm talking too much, just stop me. Just put an olive in my mouth. Plug it up. I live alone. I don't get out much. Bourbon makes me talk even more. Of course I do have the dog. I call her Amour. Yeah, that's right. Love. Pathetic, isn't it.

Tell me about you. You have cats. You live out in the woods. Well, why?—if I'm not asking too personal a question.

Sure, I can wait until after you've drunk the third martini. Drink six or seven or eight, for all I care. I don't have to be any-place. I could sit here all evening, looking out over the ocean, inhaling that air. And every once in awhile, if you don't mind my saying so, looking across the table at a lovely woman. You have the prettiest eyes. What color do you call that? Hazel? Very beautiful, if I may say so. There's something about you, a vulnerability I guess I would call it. The way you sit. The way you hold your drink. It's there. Even the way you dress. Those delicate fabrics. Maybe we should get something to eat. Stuffed mushrooms? Crabcakes? Onion rings? All right, then, the fried kalamari. I've got a little Italian in my family. I don't mind squid. No, no, really. I like it. It's not just I don't mind, I like it. I really do. You don't have to apologize. Let's get what you want. My treat. It doesn't mean we're on a date, no. It just means I feel grateful, you did such a good job, and I want to express it. No obligation. You're welcome. That's okay. That's fine.

It is calm out there today, isn't it? Not much for the surfers, I'm afraid. Nice for the lovers. Look how young those two are, strolling along with their arms around each other. Good God. Aren't they beautiful? Maybe they think this is it. He's the one. She's the one. We're in it for life. How many really make it like that?

How about you? You been married? A pretty woman like yourself, I'd lay money on it. No, no. I've talked too much already. What? Oh, hell. Oh, all right. Let me put it this way. If

they wrote an obituary on me right now, right this minute, if I
dropped dead right in the middle of this sentence, the only sur-
vivor they'd list would be my mother. She's hung in there.
That's it. No wife. No kids. And they don't put dogs in obits.
The thing is, I like it. I feel sorry for myself sometimes, but in
the end I like all the freedom. I was married once, yes. Very
young. Loved her, sure. Thought we'd have kids together, buy a
house, grow old, the works. Didn't work out. You sure the breeze
isn't too much for you? Oh, that's right, you grew up someplace
out West. Idaho? Right, right, I remember. Not Iowa, not Ohio,
but Idaho. The high desert? Nothing to stop the wind out there,
I'll bet.

Me? All over. California, Washington, New York, Virginia—
anyplace with a coast where ships could go out. I was a Navy
brat. No, I never went into the service myself. A touch of asthma.

What'd you do for fun out there?

Well, I guess high school kids everywhere do that. I know I
put down a six-pack or two, tried shots of vodka, and one reason
I don't ever drink tequila anymore is because of a vivid memory
from high school. Well, yes, I can see how hunting might be a
way of life out there. Oh sure, all teenagers are bored. You ever
kill anything? You did? What?

My ex-wife? Well, now, there's a change of subject. No, no,
that's all right. You're right—I'm not a hunter. I probably
wouldn't be all that interested in what you killed. Well, all I can
say is—she's very smart. She never missed a trick. She liked to
point out how much better things could be. Sometimes you
don't want them better. Sometimes you just—well, nevermind.
See what you do? How you get people going? Yes you do. It's the
way you sit there and listen. You'll listen to anything! Like that
woman in the workshop telling you all about her alcoholic
boyfriend. Talk about a bad situation. Jesus. Good thing she

didn't live out where you do, where there was no one to help. I'd think you'd be scared out there.

No? How come?

Well, I don't know. Maybe I would if I knew how to use it. I'm not like you. I didn't grow up hunting. So you know how to use a pistol, too? Whoa. Annie Oakley. You got a rope and a hoss there too, pardner?

Come on, I'm on my third bourbon. I can't be held responsible for everything I say. I'm sorry. No. Of course I don't think badly of you because you own a gun. I'd probably want one too if I lived out where you do. Far from the guys who answer 9-1-1. What makes me think you'd be dialing 9-1-1? Nothing. Nothing. It was just a speculation, just a what if kind of thing. If you don't mind my saying so, I think you're just a little paranoid about this gun-owning thing. Are you sure it's good for you? After all, they say people who have guns are more likely to be killed if someone actually intrudes—

No. No. I have no reason to think anyone would intrude. No. I certainly wouldn't intrude. Not unless I were invited. Then it wouldn't be intruding, would it? Anyway, how could I? I don't even know where you live. I don't even have your home phone number. I guess I could look it up— It's unlisted? Well then, I guess I couldn't look it up. Do you want to give it to me?

Well, yes, in a sense I'm your boss. Or anyway I was. But it was just for these two weeks. Now you're back working for Barb Eisenhour, as usual. Even if you weren't, couldn't I buy you dinner? It's not like I'm saying you have to have sex with me or else you lose your job. That's what sexual harassment is. Right? This isn't about sex anyway. It's just about getting to know you.

So why is your number unlisted, anyway?

Jesus. That's terrible. No wonder you're a little paranoid. No wonder. I'm sorry. I didn't realize. How well you know the guy? You did? Well, that's okay. We all make those kinds of mistakes when we're young. They don't always come back to haunt us. Lots of people date assholes, blow them off, and they actually go away. Yes, yes, that's quite a scar, though your leg is still lovely, you know, nothing to be ashamed of. He did that with a knife? You were lucky all right. You're right. If you hadn't got away—geez. Let me have your hand. That just makes me want to take care of you. I'm not a violent type, you know, but hearing what that sonofabitch did to you—it makes me want to hurt him. After all, you're not a large person. Look at the size of your wrist compared to mine. You can't weigh more than—what? One-fifteen? I'm an average sized guy and I outweigh you by at least fifty pounds. Is he a big guy?

He was six-four? Yikes. Wait a minute, what do you mean, was? Is the fucker in jail now? Is he out of your life?

What do you mean, have I ever thought of killing anybody? Of course not. What are you doing, trying to make sure I'm not the kind of guy he was? I may be confused and I may be pathetic, but I don't hit people, no.

Well, yes, I guess I did just say I wanted to hurt the guy. All right, I had a violent thought there for just a minute. If I see somebody kicking a defenseless person in the street, you think I'm going to do nothing?

And anyway what? You're not defenseless either? I can relax because—because what?

Well, I'm a little confused. Maybe it's the bourbon. Maybe we need to order some more food. I thought you kept an unlisted number because of this guy. But now I find out he's dead, gone, kaput. What happened to him anyway?

Well, sure. I can understand how you might get used to the privacy. You got used to being on the defensive, too, if you don't mind my saying so. You got used to being a little paranoid. I mean, we're not all stalkers, you know. We're not all violent animals like that. I'm not wining and dining you here just so I can get you in the sack. I resent that you brought up sexual harassment, if you want to know the truth. Jesus. I'm a decent man. I'm the kind that would figure out how to protect you from an animal like your dead stalker if I had half a chance. You remember from the cartoons, there are good guys and bad guys. I'm a good guy. I take care of my old mother and keep my dog in treats. Really, I'm all right. Trustworthy. I can hold my liquor, too. In fact, sure. Let's have another round. And some dinner too, I think. Don't you?

Okay, yes, we might think about how we're getting home. It's easy enough for me. I can take a cab. What about you? Can you get a cab way out to where you live? If not you're welcome to stay at my place. I'll sleep on the couch. I told you, I'm trustworthy. But whatever. We can see how we feel after we eat. Sometimes a person can drive just fine after the food soaks up the liquor. But you're absolutely right to think about that. No, I don't think that particular question was paranoid. No, no. It's all right. I didn't mean to criticize. I just felt—I don't know— like you were seeing me like you saw him, the stalker. Like I was some kind of animal. Oh, nothing serious. No, no. No need to be so apologetic. Jesus! Quit apologizing for yourself! It wasn't that bad. It was just for a minute. Maybe I'd feel that way too if I'd been in your shoes. Who knows?

I know it's a seafood place, but I want something beefy. A New York strip I think. You? Oh, come on. Those aren't even the main courses. Those are just the salads. My treat. Spare no expense. Go on a diet tomorrow. We're celebrating, remember? No more facing those computer-illiterates in the morning. Thank God. Now I figure you for a lobster or scallop kind of woman. Flounder's too, I don't know, ordinary for you. Crab? Nah. Not unless it was king crab, and that isn't fresh here. The lobster they fly in from Maine, I know, and it's boiled alive. Oh sorry. I guess it wasn't too appetizing to think about that. May I choose for you? Bay scallops? Right. Good choice. Light but delectable. Melt in your mouth. And local too.

Nice sunset, huh? And look, now it's dusk they're lighting the candles on the tables. Very romantic. Not to suggest anything here. After an experience like you had with that jerk, I'd be surprised if you could ever trust men again at all. By the way, what happened to him? I have to say I hope he died a horrible death.

No, I won't tell anyone. Who would I tell? My mother's 92 and in the nursing home. My dog can't talk. Oh, all right, I talk to my colleagues, but I'm not a gossip. Have I gossiped at all with you? It's not what I do. Let's face it, I'm pretty anti-social. What I'm doing here with you, this is the most conversation I've had on this level for months, maybe years. I don't remember. Oh, sure, I chat electronically, e-mail and such, but that's different. No one really knows who I am. Even if they knew my name, they wouldn't be able to watch my eyes, like I can do here with you. Or my gestures. Right now, you're getting nervous. Your eyes look kind of troubled. Still beautiful, though. See what you're doing to your napkin? You're thinking of telling me more about the shitbag who hurt you, but you're not sure. You're a little confused. Have another drink. That'll relax you. We'll be eating soon. It'll be okay. Tell me what you want to tell me, and it'll just be between you and me.

Yes, I understand, he was beating you. Good Lord, this is hard to believe, sitting across from a lovely, intelligent woman like yourself. He beat you unconscious once? I guess you're lucky to be alive. Why would he do that? Drinking? Well, sure, I guess some people react that way to alcohol. I've never been one, thank goodness. So—maybe this is a stupid question, all right?—but why didn't you leave the guy? Oh, oh of course. I'm sorry. I didn't realize. He threatened to come after you if you left. He threatened to—all right, okay, I understand. I don't need the details. What about the police? A restraining order, something like that? They wouldn't? Well, sure, I've seen those kinds of episodes on "Law and Order," things like that. But to find out someone I'm having a drink with, having dinner with, has been in that situation, well. It's different. That's all.

No, no. I don't think less of you. I'm just sorry it all happened to you. Sorry as hell. You didn't deserve it. Who knows why you got involved with a slimebag like that? They say some women just can't help it, but you're intelligent, you're attractive. You seem quite sane, in fact. I don't know how it happens. You were young, that's the way I figure it. Maybe you had a domineering father? No, we don't have to get into that. You're right.

But anyway, the jerk is dead. The wicked witch is dead. What happened to him?

Yes, I remember you saying he beat you unconscious. Sure, I remember you saying he threatened to kill you. Yes, I know, I know, you said you weren't defenseless, but the guy was six foot four. You can't be more than five foot five. Well, all right, you had that gun. Sure, a weapon like that could even things out if you knew how to use it. If you didn't panic. If he didn't wrestle it away from you and use it to—

You did? Oh. Oh my God.

Hey, get a load of that sun! Just the rim of it showing over the horizon. That's really something. That's the kind of thing I just can never get enough of. Beauty. Truth. Ha, ha. Yeah, that's me, Joe Philosopher.

No, like I said before, I've never thought of killing anyone.

My ex-wife? Oh. Well. Yes, I suppose I did think that way toward the end of my marriage. I haven't thought about this for years. I doubt if I've ever told it to anyone. I used to have this little daydream that I'd get a terminal illness and then, knowing I was going to die anyway and wouldn't have to go to prison, I'd shoot my wife. It wasn't just a daydream I had once or twice.

No, no. I never hit her. It's one thing to fantasize violence, another thing to actually—

Oh. Sorry. No. I didn't mean to criticize. You had your back to the wall, so to speak. Still, Jesus, forgive me, but it's hard to imagine. You seem so—sweet. You really thought he would kill you if you didn't—

No. No. Of course I don't blame you. You were how old? Twenty? Just a baby. Good God. I assume you got off on self-defense?

No, I guess it doesn't. Killing somebody doesn't necessarily make them go away, not entirely. My ex-wife, well, it's kind of the same thing. She's always right here, she's not gone, so to speak. Well yes, she's still alive, but in a way by telling her I wanted a divorce, I killed her. I killed my wife, you see. I made her into an ex-wife. No, of course it's not quite the same as making her into a corpse, but maybe it has some of the same elements.

You don't think you'd do it again, do you?

Because I really like you, but I'd hate to think— I mean, I don't see how I could forget— Yes, sure, I can see how it would be hard to know when to bring it up, when to spill the beans, so to speak. Jesus.

What kind of gun do you have? Oh yeah? That's a handgun, right? You carry it with you? Right there in your purse, is it? Jesus. So where do you get something like that?

Oh no. I'm just curious. Hearing your story, it makes me wonder about the various details. It makes me think. Is there a place where they teach you to use those things? No, I guess you wouldn't. Sure. You learned all you needed to know as a kid popping bottles in the desert. Well, I guess that turned out to be lucky for you. Not so lucky for your boyfriend. Not that I blame you at all.

So you liked the scallops? Good. I'm glad. I'm relieved, in fact. I want you to have a good time here, you know. I want you to be happy. Your happiness has always been important to me. Yes, my steak is just fine. I think I just drank too much to be very hungry. Good idea. A doggy bag. You're right. Amour would love it. She'd be very grateful. That's very thoughtful of you.

You know, Amour would probably like living out in the country. She'd be a good watch dog out there. She barks at anything. Boy, does she bark. And you know, if someone were to come in, a stranger, even a woman, I think she'd attack. She's a springer spaniel—not huge—but she could do some damage.

You'd like to meet her? Well, yes, I did say I would sleep on the couch. Sure thing. We can just—oh! Jesus! Shit! I just remembered. My cousin's supposed to come in late tonight. He sells software, you know, like a traveling salesman, and tomorrow he has to show his stuff down here. He's driving from Boston. I guess I could sleep on the floor, but—you know, Amour knows my cousin, but I'm not sure how she'd be with you. She's a little vicious toward strangers sometimes. She hasn't been around many women either. Except my mother of course.

Yeah, I guess another time would be better. Let me put some money toward your cab ride home. After all, I'm the one that got you shnockered.

No. No, you're absolutely right. You made that decision yourself. I don't have to take responsibility for it, do I? Still it's a habit, I admit. You're so tiny compared to me. Like a child. It's hard to remember you're—

My home phone number? Sure. You can find it in the book. Although I have to say, I like the idea of getting an unlisted number. You probably don't get as many sales calls that way, right? Sounds good. So if you call and the number's changed, that's what's going on.

So. You okay? Good, good. Sure. A walk on the beach will clear your head some. It's dark out now, but you'll be all right. You have—well—your purse with you.

Me? No. I better get home. Now that I've remembered my cousin, I better go home and clean up. He might come early. It's been great, terrific, it really has. I think you're amazing. I'll never forget you, believe that. Oh sure, sure, we'll see each other around. No, no. I said it was my treat, and I meant it. I'll get the tab. You have a good walk, and be careful. Yes, sure. I'm sober now. The meat sobered me up. I'm sober as a judge now. Plenty sober.

SWIMMERS

DOROTHY COOVER, RESIDENT BIOLOGIST, was driving a Fish and Wildlife Service Jeep to the Necropsy Lab when she passed the building where the animals were sacrificed and saw all the cooperative education students sitting in the back of a green truck, their rubber boots up to their knees and their heads bowed. Her lover Lenny Moore, the tall young man from Virginia, stood in the pick-up bed, his back against the cab of the truck, clasping his hands in front of him as if he were about to be led to the gas chamber himself. Dorothy swung left, pulling her Jeep next to the truck, and said, "What's going on?"

The students looked up. There were five in all—Lenny, who had been assigned to Roger Harkin, the raptor man; Sharla, a sweet little blonde from University of Maryland, Dorothy's own charge; and three from Endangered Species whose names Dorothy couldn't recall.

Lenny swung down from the pick-up bed and put his hands on the passenger door of Dorothy's Jeep. He bent like a willow. His hair, the color of tree bark in shadow, fell forward over his shoulders, and he smiled, revealing what Dorothy felt were endearingly crooked teeth. Lenny glanced at his watch, then spoke back over his shoulder. "They're finished." He seemed to be in charge.

One of the other young men—Bob? Bruce? whoever he was, he was dark, dressed in cut-offs and a tank top, his arms and chest muscular and furred—jumped down from the truck, turned the wheel on the carbon monoxide tank to shut it off, and opened the door of the shed. Inside were crates of mallards, all of them dead. The girls hopped out of the truck now, too, to load the crates into the pick-up. In their shorts and halter-tops, attire Dorothy and the other biologists allowed because of the heat, they looked like they were ready for a stroll on an ocean-front boardwalk. Only the rubber boots, footwear for pens layered in duck shit, gave them away. Dorothy herself was more modestly dressed—knee-length shorts, sleeveless blouse. She rubbed one hand up and down over the opposite arm. It was firm, because she worked out: every morning, she jogged along the path by the river that cut through the research center, fighting what would otherwise be a natural decline. Her husband Tom, on the other hand, had let himself go.

"With a little effort, you could have your old body back," she'd told him.

He'd smiled, opened the jar of peanuts he was holding, shaken some into his open palm and tossed them into his mouth. Then lifted his shirt and slapped his big gut joyfully.

Lenny, like the other cooperative education students, wore cut-offs and a tank top, revealing a dark, even tan and the long musculature of a swimmer. He even made love like a swimmer, moving deep inside her with strong, rhythmic thrusts. They used the cot upstairs in Dorothy's building after hours. Last time—in fact, last night—the yellow light of dusk had come in through the Venetian blinds, stippling the room as if she and Lenny were underwater. Dorothy wasn't much of a swimmer, though with Lenny she had felt she could learn.

But it was August. Only a few days left before Lenny returned to college. The co-op students worked six months on jobs in their fields, then went to school for six months. Lenny was 23, a senior; this was his last co-op stint. Dorothy was 37. Tom, a statistician, worked across the research center—two locked gates and numerous animal pens between him and his wife.

She'd visualized the scene of Tom's outrage, had panicky periods when every ring of the phone made her want to confess, sure one of her lovers would call, a la "Fatal Attraction"—a movie she was sorry she'd ever seen—to tell Tom what had happened, to ruin her life. And there had been medical scares. The time she'd thought she was pregnant, she wouldn't have known with whose baby; the time she'd finally—after the second lover—had an AIDS test. Normally it was hard, when she was in the first throes of passion, for her not to despise Tom. There were things about him that were so . . . to put it kindly, unattractive. For instance, he had a habit of sniffing, when he was concentrating hard, that made her want to scream. A way of putting his hands on her shoulders when they were at parties that felt like ownership. And there were little things he shouldn't be asked to change—clipping his toenails into the sink, crumpling his towel over the bathroom rack, leaving a fine film of bath powder over everything . . . it was idiotic that such things should bother her…and his sense of humor, though it had been one of his prime attractions for her, was sometimes inappropriate. After the breast lump had been found, for instance, but before the biopsy, he'd tried to cheer her by talking about how she'd look as a Picasso: cut-up. Fortunately the lump was benign, but it had further convinced her that it was important to be living, by which she meant not missing chances, such as the chance she had with Lenny.

She'd noticed him last year among the new crop of co-ops

partly because he was tall and lean but also because unlike the other students, he didn't act shy around the biologists.

"It's hard to believe the kid's 22," Roger-the-Raptor-Man, as the co-op students called him, had said last year. "He's incredibly savvy."

This year Roger had lent Lenny to Dorothy one day when both her co-ops were ill. The two of them worked quietly taking blood samples, Lenny pinning each duck to the metal table and holding its wing while Dorothy worked the needle.

Afterwards, as they were washing up, Lenny said, "You're impressive."

"Why?"

"You're not squeamish. I've seen some of the others mutilate the veins because they were afraid they'd hurt the animal."

Dorothy shrugged. "I guess you get over that. You have to."

Lenny stood in the lab watching her dry her hands. The lab was in a building next to the duck pens. From there it was a long walk to the offices on the other side of a locked gate. Lenny and Dorothy were alone. When she turned away from the sink, she could see that he admired her. But, she told herself, he was the student, she was the supervisor; it could mean her job.

Later, though, it occurred to her that he was Roger's student. She wasn't his direct supervisor at all. They passed each other on the Center's roads at least once a day. Leaning out of their open Jeeps, they slapped each other's palms and laughed. Sometimes stopped, engines idling, to chat. Eventually met for lunch. Then walks after work. The first time they made love, it was in the woods. On a bed of moss, he pulled off her pants. She helped, giggling. Then lay back. He stroked the long, soft hair between her legs, then moved it aside to kiss her there. She looked up at the sky through the pines and said, as if speaking to God, "Thank you."

The feeling of gratitude stayed with her, convincing her—

oddly enough—that Lenny was helping her to love Tom more. She was able to come home, after a night with Lenny, and kiss Tom with real affection. She imagined herself like the doves in the Songbird House allowed to fly free while the students cleaned their cages. It wasn't much trouble getting the doves to come back; they returned on their own, feeling safer in their cages.

* * *

But now Lenny indicated the truck and the crew, so recently sitting in the bed of the pick-up. "We just wanted to have a moment of silence for the ducks." He shrugged his shoulders. "We all know it has to be done, but we have our feelings about it. I wouldn't want you to think we were slacking off."

She tried to read his face. Was he saying this for the benefit of the others? Surely he didn't really worry about her judgment of his work. Nevertheless, the way Lenny was looking at her, his eyes full of compassion for the animals, Dorothy was touched. She licked her lips and swallowed. She fingered her hair, felt it frizzing in the humid heat, and was sorry. She, too, liked the ducks. Their friendly faces. Their beautiful heads, especially the males with those sleek green feathers. She didn't like to sacrifice them, but she and other biologists at the Maryland station were feeding small amounts of oil to the mallards. They wanted to know the effects of oil spills so they could help the mallards' wild cousins. To judge the effects, they had to look at the internal organs. "It's no problem," she told Lenny. "It's only natural to feel sorry."

The word sorry made her think how last night, when they'd been in the room with the cot, he'd said she was the first woman he'd ever really loved.

"We're so happy together," he'd said, as if he were arguing.

"So right."

"Yes," she'd said. Then, waving her hand to indicate the cot, the room, the building. "But these are only experimental conditions. What would happen to us in the wild?"

"If there were predators," he'd said, nuzzling her breasts, "I'd protect you."

She leaned down, cupping his testicles in her hands, kissing them. "Bird eggs," she'd said. "Delicate and beautiful as bird eggs. If we were wild birds, we'd probably step on something precious in the nest."

Lenny pulled her up by one arm, roughly, so that she pushed his hand away and said, "Ouch." He pinned her to the bed, holding her shoulders, his hair grazing her face. "Bad things can happen in captivity, too." When he let go, he turned away, curling protectively, knees to his chest.

Trying to make him feel better, she'd suggested they meet for weekend trysts after he went back to school. But he was young, she'd reminded him. She didn't want their involvement to mean he might miss finding someone with whom he could spend his life. "Eventually you'll have to give me up," Dorothy had said, and tried to smile.

* * *

When she had got home from her evening with Lenny, she had slipped into bed next to Tom. The ceiling fan's blades cut the air, uh-wmm, uh-wmm. She laced her fingers across her chest. Tom wriggled deeper into his pillow. Although he was turned away from her, she could see the familiar curve of one ear. She was no longer amazed that he couldn't tell when she'd been with another man. Years ago, it had enraged her—especially with her first lover. She'd felt Tom slipping away from her then, spending more and more of his energy on his dissertation, and she guessed his withdrawal fed her sense that she deserved to do what she was doing, that she had a right to it.

It was hard to believe, now, that she had fallen for the sleepy-eyed musician who had played his guitar by a pond on the edge of campus. The songs were sweet and sad. Now she couldn't remember any of the words—only the feeling of longing, the music tugging at her viscera. She was, after all, only an animal like the ducks with their slippery intestines, their sleek brown livers. After a few sessions, Russ asked to read her palm. He took her hand and said, "I knew it. See all these lines? It means you're an old soul." The come-on seemed ridiculous to her now. But when he kissed her hand, his mustache tickling, he broke some barrier of space. They embraced for awhile, then walked to his van. He drove onto a secluded road and pulled over. She was frightened. When they actually made love, she couldn't relax, and it was slightly painful. Afterwards, though, Russ stroked her hair, kissed her forehead, and massaged her feet. He was married, too. He said the first time he tried to sleep with another woman, he couldn't.

"Her name was Dorothy, too," he said. "I've never forgotten her. You're like my second chance."

She got home late, but Tom was still at the library. She imagined him in his cubicle reading about standard deviations, glad to note that she could see the irony in this, that her sense of humor was intact. She took a shower and washed away the smell of Russ. Then she lay naked on the bed and thought of Russ's fingers in her hair and his body over hers and the feel of him moving inside her. It was like falling from a cliff.

In the morning, she found Tom sleeping soundly beside her. Nothing was different. She got up and made coffee. Tom came into the kitchen, sliced a bagel, and put it in the toaster.

"Get a lot done last night?" she asked.

"Not enough, goddamnit." He rubbed his hand over his face.

"I have to go right back to it this morning."

She hugged him, but he pushed her gently aside and said, "Coffee."

Eventually, of course, Tom had finished his PhD and they'd both got the jobs at the research center two states away. She and Russ said good-bye. Good-bye was, they agreed, built into the contract, as it was with John, her second lover, whom she met a year later and who, after a few months, drifted away.

Extramarital sex was, she thought now, lifting her hands up to the air that was pushed down over her body by the fan blades, a kind of drug. The air felt good. She threw off the sheets. Tom stirred and flung an arm across her stomach.

"You smell clean," he mumbled.

She'd taken a shower after she and Lenny made love. The shower was next to the cot in her building, in a room meant for biologists whose experiments had to be tended through the night.

"I took a shower," she said.

He touched the calf of her leg with the ball of his foot. "Um."

She put the flat of her hand on Tom's naked chest. She'd massaged Lenny's chest earlier, tracing the line of dark hair from his belly to his groin, then lightly stroking his penis until she took it into her mouth. Now she moved her hand down between Tom's legs. There had been nights when she'd made love to Tom after she'd been with Lenny. Lenny made her feel beautiful, passionate. She'd slide into bed next to Tom and massage him, kissing his neck, his chest, then get on top. She'd lift her breasts, stroke her nipples with her fingers.

But now, depressed by Lenny's impending departure, she let her hand fall away. Tom turned over. She curled into his back, comforted by his big, inert body.

* * *

She could not yet smell the ducks, but soon, in this heat, she would. They would take the animals to the Necropsy Lab. The students would pluck them. She and Roger would remove the livers, examine and weigh them. When they shouted out weights, the students would record them, one sheet for each animal, identifying them by the tags on their webbed orange feet.

Sharla was crying as she loaded the crates. Lenny looked at her, then at his hands, then back at Dorothy, stricken.

"I'm sorry it has to be done," Dorothy said.

Lenny came toward Dorothy with a crate in his arms; the green head of a mallard emerged, its beak hanging open.

None of the co-op students would look her in the eye.

"I'll meet you at the lab," she said to the group of them, to Lenny, although he didn't look up. She put the Jeep in gear and drove down the lane. Early morning steam rose from the road, and trees arched overhead, closing out the sky with their branches. Only 9 a.m., but already it was an effort to breathe. When she scratched her cheek, oil from her skin caked beneath her fingernails. At least the Necropsy Lab would be air-conditioned. The Jeep roared. With the pedal to the floor, it only did 35 mph. Through the open sides she could see the forest, viney and tangled, whizzing by; if she'd been here earlier, no doubt she'd have seen deer. There were several thousand acres in the refuge. There was more than one small herd of deer, occasional foxes, beavers, otters. Even, once, a bobcat. But in this heat the animals were probably already bedded down, possibly unconscious. It was the only way to escape.

The road divided, and suddenly, where she should have gone left, she found herself, without planning to, veering right, taking a detour by the eagle pens. Across from the eagle pens the resident behaviorist had built an observation tower. In the top was room enough for two to sit shoulder to shoulder, watching through binoculars and taking notes. Lenny had spent hours there, documenting the birds' nesting rituals on his own time. She'd been there with him once or twice.

It was common for the co-op students to become attached to a particular species. Sharla, for instance, was trying to raise Louisiana heron chicks which otherwise would be killed. Biologists from the Gulf sent Dorothy the heron eggs. She put them in the incubator, coating them with a drop of oil every day. When, despite the oil, they hatched, she had no use for the heron chicks—nor, she had argued with Sharla—any way to raise them. But she had agreed to let Sharla get an old heat lamp out of a shed and set up a cage for six of them. Sharla had to feed them from an eye-dropper five times a day, at least. Dorothy didn't think the chicks would live, but she always tried to give the co-op students the opportunity to find things out for themselves. She could understand Sharla's horror at the manner in which the chicks were dispatched: in a sealed jar with a wad of cotton coated in chloroform. To demonstrate to Sharla that she understood what was involved in killing them, Dorothy had accompanied her to the incubator room for the first slaughter this year. In the palm of Dorothy's hand, each day-old chick had trembled, warm and utterly vulnerable. It wasn't as if, despite her years of experience, Dorothy didn't feel anything when she put each chick into the jar, sealed the lid, and—eyes averted—felt it thumping the sides of the jar trying to get out. And then, to take the little bodies to the incinerator and toss them in, as if they were no more than offal, as if they hadn't—just now—lived. It wasn't as if it didn't affect her.

She turned off the Jeep and listened to the eagles calling back and forth. She climbed into the observation tower. How did things look to Lenny from here? What was it like to live in his young, strong body? To believe, watching the eagles mate, in true love? Though the air in the tower was stiflingly close, and her skin was already coated with perspiration, Dorothy watched the birds. The female sat on the nest, her wings slightly outspread, looking ragged. The male flew to the floor of the pen, picked up a dead rat, and flew back to the perch, tearing off meat. Still clutching part of the rat in his claw (Dorothy could see the white tail looping over the perch), he hopped toward the female, bent his head to hers and fed her some meat. It was too bad for the rat, but the birds were magnificent.

* * *

Roger-the-Raptor-Man who was, despite the air-conditioning, heavily perspiring, had already begun the dissections in the Necropsy Lab. Lenny was assisting. They wore white lab coats over their clothes. Dorothy had come in through the door from the hallway. The other co-op students sat on the loading dock out back—Dorothy could see them through the back door—plucking the birds' breasts.

"Ah, Dorothy," Roger said, wiggling his eyebrows. "This isn't Oz." He looked up from the duck he was cutting, holding his gloved hands up like a surgeon's. The birds were laid out on shiny metal tables, lights shining onto the open cavities of their breasts. Roger's round glasses caught the light, and he wore a comical expression. Lenny kept his back turned, but she glanced at the naked backs of his legs emerging from beneath the lab coat.

She put on her rubber gloves and lab coat, then brushed her bangs out of her face. Her hair was cut short in a kind of bob, the back of her neck shaved. She stood in front of the air condition-er for a moment, letting it cool her, picked up a scalpel and approached the metal table, coming up next to Lenny. His hair hung on either side of his face; she couldn't read his expression. She adjusted the lamp so that it shone more directly onto the bird's plucked breast. Roger had already moved to the other table and called Sharla in to assist him, leaving Lenny with Dorothy.

Dorothy sliced open the bird and peeled the flesh back from the breastbone, revealing the organs. The bird was still warm. She located the liver, removed it deftly, and put it onto the scale. She read out the weight. Lenny glanced at the bird's leg band, recorded the number, then placed the carcass into a garbage bag. Eventually it, like the heron chicks, would go into the incinerator.

The loading dock out back was heaped with birds. In this group, there were 250. There would be three other groups, for a total of 1,000 birds. It was important, Roger and she had agreed—and Tom, as statistician, had concurred—to have a decent sample size.

"What a waste," Lenny muttered, putting another carcass into the bag.

Dorothy clenched her teeth and cut into another bird. The more quickly they could get this over with, the better for all of them. Didn't Lenny think she had feelings, too, about this? Did he really think she enjoyed the stink of dead birds, her hands in their open cavities, their still-warm livers sliding around in her fingers? It was hardly appetizing . . . yet she kept glancing at Lenny's legs, the swell of his hips beneath the lab coat. Even when she willed herself to focus on the work, her body was aware of his, as if her cells had become magnetized and Lenny's held the opposite charge. She kept shifting away from him, sighing deeply to release her frustration, then yawning as animals sometimes, she knew, did when they saw a thing they wanted but couldn't have. It was called displacement behavior.

You are so beautiful, she kept saying, silently, to Lenny. His thick, slightly waved, dark hair; his big long-fingered hands; his dark, smooth skin—skin, she had told him, like an Indian's, smooth from his throat to his hairless chest to his bellybutton, where the black line of fur began. His eyes were the surprise: a blue so pale they were almost gray. They gave him an eerie look that Dorothy found exciting. But now he stood beside her, the shoulder-length hair still shielding his face, his body turned away from hers, resisting.

And why shouldn't he? She had had to remind him of their circumstances. Of what was real. Of what he'd known all along. Certain limitations.

For a while they worked in relative silence, Roger or Dorothy calling out an occasional weight, Sharla or Lenny saying, "Okay," or "Got it." The air conditioner, an old model, roared. Dorothy, standing in front of it, had goose bumps.

Then Roger called out a weight, and Sharla said in a strangled voice, "Oh, no. It's number 34." She turned away from the table, stripped off her rubber gloves and threw them into the plastic garbage bag by Roger's table. Tears streamed down her face. "I'm sorry," she said, and ran out the door that led to the hallway.

"What's the problem?" Roger asked, his hands in mid-air.

Lenny looked at Dorothy then, for the first time since she'd come in, and in his look was a world of blame. "She loved that bird," he said.

Roger said in an accusing voice, "She knew it had to go."

Lenny shook his head, drawing his lids down over his fierce eyes—blink, blink—like the eagle's. Then he, too, drew off the rubber gloves and cast them into the garbage sack. "I'll see what I can do for her."

The other co-op students went on plucking; they hadn't heard. But Roger opened the back door. "Buddy?" That was the dark, muscular student's name—not Bruce or Bob. "Buddy? We need you in here."

Buddy got up from the loading dock, dropping his plucked bird into the pile. "Where'd everybody go?" he asked, glancing in through the door.

Roger shook his head. "It's hard to sacrifice these birds," he said to the other students. "Especially if you get attached to one. But we've got to get these livers out while the birds are fresh. If you're going to have feelings about it, try to have them later, okay?" He looked at the two remaining students, two girls from Endangered Species—both in shorts and halter tops, one slim, the other heavy, both of them brunette. He glanced at Dorothy. "Which one do you want?"

The smell of ducks decaying rapidly in the heat wafted in through the door—a sour, overwhelming stench. Dorothy's stomach heaved; she tasted bile. Heat came into the door in waves. The laboratory appeared to be moving. Both of the women looked impossibly young. One of them opened her mouth like a fledgling's. What were their names—Melanie? Melinda?

"You all right, Dot?" Roger took her under one elbow.

She closed her eyes.

"Shut the door," Roger said to Buddy. "Help me get her to a chair."

The two of them supported Dorothy, leading her to a metal folding chair. Roger told her to put her head between her legs.

The other co-op students came in, too. She could see their legs surrounding her, then heard another door open and close and saw the legs of Lenny and Sharla approaching as they returned; Lenny's voice asking, "What's going on?" Roger's hand on her shoulder. Then Lenny's, briefly cool on the back of her neck.

"Do you want me to call Tom?" Roger asked.

The tiles on the floor were smeared with blood, and

Dorothy's bloody gloves were still on her hands. She stripped them off, then put her hands to her forehead. One of the girls from Endangered Species bent, retrieved the gloves, and tossed them into the garbage.

"I'll call your husband," Roger said.

She gripped Roger's hand, still on her shoulder, and shook her head. She raised herself up, sitting straight, and looked at Lenny. He seemed to be at a great height, but he bent his knees and came down to her level. She felt a ripping sensation inside her chest.

"Breathe," Lenny said.

Roger's hand disappeared from her shoulder, but the co-op students still surrounded her, forming a protective circle. Lenny leaned his forehead into hers. She wanted to speak, to say she was sorry, she loved him, she couldn't give him up, but it was as if a great hand were forcing the words back down her throat.

Sharla said, "I think she's trying to talk."

But Lenny touched his fingertips to Dorothy's lips. "Shhh. Shhh." He glanced at the other students. His fingers were cool on Dorothy's bare shoulders as he stood up. Leaning her forehead into his belly, she felt her heart fling itself against her ribs.

"What's wrong with her?" Sharla asked.

"I don't know," Lenny said. "I think she just needs to regulate her body temperature. Being out in this heat, then coming back in . . . maybe the conditions changed too fast." He moved behind Dorothy, rubbing her back, then cupping his hands at the base of her neck. "Just relax."

She leaned back, letting him hold her head, chin upraised as if she were floating. When she opened her eyes, she saw Lenny's face outlined against the white ceiling. She wanted to reach for him, but her arms, as in a dream, were too heavy to lift, and already he seemed far away, like a life raft at the top of a swell on the horizon.

BLACK ICE

—for Carol

ANNA GAZED DOWN THE MOUNTAIN along the narrow road, in the direction of the highway. A few strong men could easily lift the little car—a Honda Accord—back onto the road, out of the snowbank it had ploughed into while Beth was driving. It hadn't been Beth's fault. It had been stupid of them to try to get down the mountain, given the ice. It was black ice, the invisible kind through which you could see the harmless-looking pavement, the kind you don't even know you've hit until your car spins out of control and no pumping of brake or steering of wheel can save you. The car had spun once, twice, and while it was spinning Anna had had time to wonder what she could do to help Beth, who was exuding a Zen-like calm, who was steering into the spin, as was correct, concentrating so hard that Anna decided the best thing to do was not interfere, try to relax; she'd heard that if you relaxed, the impact of head-on-windshield or feet-against-carpet, driving the shinbones into the knees, wouldn't be as bad: it was resisting that stiffened you, turning your bones into brittle sticks.

Beth had understood, when the car spun the first time—as if tweaked by a giant finger—that she had hit black ice; that the road, however, was not terribly treacherous, a high soft bank of snow on either side and luckily no other traffic: no one to hit, to hurt. Only herself and Anna in a car that, going as slowly as they were, would at the worst get stuck in a snowbank. Still, the second spin surprised her; she forgot to turn into it. She saw that they were going over the edge of the road. She jerked her right arm up, meaning to prevent Anna's body from hitting the windshield.

The car ploughed, nose first, into a soft snowbank. There was a jolt; their seat belts held. Neither felt anything more than the bumps they'd endured when the car hit several exceptionally deep potholes on the way up the mountain. Now they were left with the mess: the stuck car, the falling snow, the cold. A mess as banal as the mess Anna had tried to escape by driving to the top of the mountain that very afternoon.

Beth was already outside, walking up the hill into the woods, cracking branches, stuffing them under the tires. Anna would have to help, though she was still wet and cold from their hike at the top of the mountain, her jacket dripping, her cheap nylon wind pants clinging to her legs. Unlike Beth, she wore sneakers, not snow boots. She stepped into the snow, meaning to climb up the bank for more branches, but Beth said, "Are you crazy? You're not dressed for this. You just stay put. Get ready to drive the car when I get the stuff under the wheels."

"I could go to the highway for help," Anna said.

"In that get-up?" Beth snorted. "The highway's at least ten miles. Let's just give this a try first." Beth lay one set of sticks in parallel lines behind the tires, then put a second set across them and perpendicular to the first. If she'd driven her own truck, she'd be wrapping wire from the winch around a tree and cranking the wheels out of the ditch. Why had she allowed Anna to take this piece of shit car up into the mountains? Anna didn't even carry chains or a shovel. She probably hadn't thought to put a sleeping bag into the trunk. Beth should've checked on that, but the forecast had said rain, not snow. It had been fifty degrees when they left the valley.

Anna watched her through the beating wipers. Beth wore a red parka and form-fitting ski pants. Her abbreviated hair stuck out in silvery curls from beneath her ski cap. If it weren't for the gray, Anna thought, Beth would look like an adolescent boy gleefully playing with sticks in the snow. She clambered up and down the bank into the trees, hunting the right twigs. Then she came up to the car and tapped on Anna's window. Anna rolled it down.

"You rock the car back and forth while I push. When I give the signal, put it in reverse and floor it."

"Look at this stuff." Anna said out the window, pointing to the sky. The snow had turned to ice.

"Tell me about it," Beth said, rubbing her exposed neck. "It hurts."

"You really think this is going to work?" Anna asked.

Beth shrugged.

* * *

Resting her forehead on the steering wheel, despairing at Beth's last failed effort—tires spinning on the branches she'd arranged to give them traction, nose of the car too deep in the ditch to push itself out, Anna asked, "What are we going to do? Do you think we should try to walk out?"

Beth glanced at her watch. "I figure we have another hour, hour-and-a-half, of light."

"I have a flashlight in here." Anna reached across Beth's lap, opening the glove box. She rummaged through papers, toothpicks, plastic toys, until she found a palm-sized white plastic flashlight. "It's small, but—" She switched it on and off several times; no light appeared. She shook it, opened the battery compartment and gazed inside. "Got any Double As?"

Ice came down more heavily from the sky, hitting the roof of the car and the windshield like chunks of gravel.

Beth shook her head, looking at Anna's sneakers, her cotton shirt, her thin pants. "You're just not dressed for this." Anna parted her lips as if to reply. Her teeth were straight and even. Silky blonde hair fell across her shoulders. Even in crisis, Beth thought, she was lovely, though her neck had recently begun to wrinkle, and for a few years her large breasts had sagged. Still, because of her round dimpled cheeks and her big blue Alice-in-Wonderland eyes, she gave off the sweet trusting confidence of a child, a quality that made Beth feel alternately protective and burdened.

"I just can't believe it," Anna said. "It was so nice at the top. God, when that sun came out—"

"You were right about that view. That was a great view."

"Not something worth spending the night for, though."

Beth glanced around the car. The back seat was a jumble of student papers and crumpled trash, McDonald's cups, plastic wrappers, a bag of cat food. "Any chance you have a blanket or a sleeping bag in the trunk?"

Anna shook her head. "Afraid not."

"Matches?"

Anna pointed to the hole where the lighter used to plug into the dashboard. "That made a great toy for Jason when he was still in his car seat. As long as it wasn't hot, of course. It disappeared a few years ago."

"How much gas in the tank?"

"I was planning to fill up on the way home."

"Okay." Beth clenched her teeth. "Let me think." The car

was still running, heat blasting from the vents, so they were comfortable. But Beth considered Anna's stupid little sneakers and cotton socks; they'd been soaked through as she walked on the ridge. Most of what Anna had on, if not completely wet, was—at the least—not warm. Once they turned off the car, Anna would start to shiver. It wouldn't take long for the temperature inside the car to drop to the temperature outside, though at least they'd be protected from the wind.

"I was trying to prove I was just as competent as Eric," Anna said. "I heard him talking about this place with one of his Forest Service buddies, and I thought—that's the kind of place I love, but normally I'd wait for Eric to take me. Then I thought, grow up. Why not find it on the map and drive there myself?"

"At least you didn't come up here alone," Beth said. "Although who knows? If you'd been driving, we might be on the highway by now."

Anna leaned her head on Beth's shoulder. "You hit a patch of black ice, you're going to lose control. I'm just glad it didn't happen up higher, where we would've sailed off the edge of the mountain and rolled."

Beth resisted the impulse to gather Anna into her lap where Ellen used to fit, her back against Beth's front, her head in the crook of Beth's arm, Beth's arms around her. The television lulled them to sleep until Beth heard the locks click on the front door, then smelled the cigarettes that meant Mommy home in her short black skirt and white blouse, hair curled around her face, eyelashes black with mascara and black under her eyes, too, lips outlined red, nails glittering with polish, pale neck giving way to the mysterious shadow between her breasts, outlined by the white ruffles of her uniform.

"Time for bed." Mommy switched off the television and gathered Ellen in her arms, carrying Ellen to her mattress on the floor of the single bedroom. Beth stood at the door as her mother pulled the covers over her sleeping sister and then Beth climbed onto the twin mattress next to Ellen's, against the opposite wall, too big now—unlike Ellen—to be tucked in. Then there was the steady rhythm of Ellen's breathing, the TV again, faintly, in the next room, the smoke from Mommy's cigarettes, the jingling of change as Mommy counted up her tips, and finally the darkness after the lamp and the TV went off by the couch.

"Hope you didn't have a hot date planned tonight," Anna said.

"It's Paul's and Eva's twenty-fifth anniversary. They're going out to dinner at Giovanni's."

Anna squeezed her hand. "Don't take this wrong, but I don't know how you stand that. I mean, I know they have an understanding. But still, you're not the wife. You don't get priority. It would make me crazy."

"Priority means commitment. Not something I'm interested in." Beth withdrew her hand to glance at her watch again, then leaned over to check the gas gauge. "Shit."

"I know. I should've filled up before we left."

"I think we ought to conserve it. Turn it off for awhile, until we get really cold again."

"Okay." Anna switched off the engine.

"I'd say I'd walk out, but I know there's no way I'm making ten miles before dark, and in this stuff," she pointed out the window at the falling ice, "I don't want to take my chances." She took a deep breath. "Did you tell anybody where you were going?"

Anna shook her head. "Eric might wonder when I don't call Jason tonight. But he'll probably figure I'm avoiding him or something." She looked out the window. "Did I tell you he took out a year's lease on that apartment?"

"Oh no."

"So I guess he's serious. I guess he means to stay away."

Beth touched her shoulder. "Oh honey."

"He takes Jason to school tomorrow, and then Jason just gets off the bus at home in the afternoon." Anna sat up. "Shit! What if I'm not there?"

Beth put her arm around Anna, pulling her close. She closed her eyes, remembering the narrow road between them and the highway, mile after mile of curves and hills. "Worst case scenario, we spend the night here, and in the morning I walk out, get help, and we get out of here."

Beth could make time, all right. Anna had hiked with her before. When she got to the highway, Beth could flag down a ride, get to a phone and call Eric. Anna squeezed Beth's hand. "God, I'm glad you're here."

"I'd like to say the same, but," Beth gestured out the window, "this isn't exactly my idea of a good time."

For awhile they listened to the ice chattering on the roof of the car. The air was white with fog, gray trunks of trees mere shadows now, barely visible through the mist. Anna shifted, pulling away from Beth.

"Eric and Jason are probably playing pool in the game room at his apartment complex right now. They're probably having a good time. They're having such a fucking good time they aren't even thinking about me. They don't even need me. They're just fine."

Beth noted Anna's pinched expression, her hunched posture against the car door. "Now honey. That's what you want," Beth said. "You want him to be comfortable with his dad. You want him to be happy. I wish it'd been like that for me as a kid. Two good people like you and Eric looking after us all the time."

"I know. It could be worse. But it was so much better before Eric split."

Beth touched Anna's hand. "The fucking jerk."

* * *

They huddled together as darkness settled into the woods around them, the trees blackening first, the spaces between the trees filling in with darkness, balls of ice still raining down, pinging against the roof of the car, weighting the tree limbs. A sleepiness settled over Anna. Beth smelled of apples. Maybe her shampoo. The down of her parka made a comfortable pillow. She imagined a fire crackling in a big fireplace at a ski lodge. There were people who would have chosen to go up to a resort instead of driving on a Forest Service road, who would've got stuck in style during an ice storm, who would've been soaking, now, in a hot tub. She felt Beth's body relax, her head on Anna's suddenly grow heavy. They'd both have stiff necks. There was Eric, trudging up the road through the snow in his Bermuda shorts, tanned and healthy, and she was saying, "Did you bring Jason? Did you pick him up?" and now the three of them were down by the creek hunting for crawdads, but the fish stood up on its tail and spoke—saying what?—she leaned forward to make it out. Its gills heaved. She worried that it would drown. There was a landslide, rocks tumbling from the slope above Jason, the sound of them explosive, like cannons. Anna was lying down on the riverbank. She had to get up.

"Oh, motherfucker," Beth said.

"What?" Anna sat up. There had been a sound, an explosion, something, she didn't know...

"Oh, Ellen."

"What?"

Beth began to cry. "I remember that sound."

"No," Anna said. She peered into the darkness. They were on the mountain. They'd been driving down, Beth had, and the car hit black ice. They were stuck in a snowbank. There was an ice storm. But they were all right. "No, I heard it, too."

Another explosion made them both scream.

"Jesus Christ," Beth said.

Anna tightened her arms around Beth. "It's like a war zone."

Beth pushed Anna away and wrenched the car door open, pushing it hard against the wind.

"What are you doing?"

Anna grabbed her friend's arm before Beth could climb out of the car, reaching across to pull the car door shut. "Are you out of your mind?"

Beth struggled. "Let me go."

"Are you crazy?"

Another explosion sounded, and this time they felt the earth vibrate, the car rocking as a tree hit the ground.

Beth started to push the door open again; Anna hadn't been able to close it all the way. Anna was shivering now, her teeth chattering. Once again she reached across Beth's lap to hold the door closed. Beth pushed her away, leaned against the door. When the cold air rushed in, though, Beth recoiled, shaking her head as if to clear it, as if she were dazed.

"Beth, stop it!" Anna yelled. "I'm fucking freezing."

Beth closed the door, then rubbed her hands over her face in a scrubbing motion. "Oh shit. I was dreaming. I thought the trees—" Beth indicated the darkness outside "—the sound of them falling, I thought it was a gunshot. I thought—" her voice caught in a sob. "I thought it was Ellen. I must have been dreaming. How long have we been asleep?" She pushed a button on her watch that lit the dial. "Jesus fucking Christ. It's two in the morning." She turned to Anna. "Look how you're shivering. We better turn on the engine. Get a blast of heat."

Anna held one hand over the fingers of the other, trying to make them grasp and turn the key.

"I'll get it," Beth said. She turned the key. Nothing. Tried again, thought she could hear a faint click. "Don't panic." She turned the key to off, took a deep breath, turned it again.

"It couldn't be out of gas already."

"I think it's the battery," Beth said. "I think the battery's gone dead. Do you know anything about the battery?"

Anna shook her head. "Why would you go out there?"

"I told you, I wasn't awake. I thought that sound was a gunshot. I was dreaming, dreaming of Ellen."

"You were just a kid."

"I know." Beth hit the dashboard with her fist and slumped forward. "How about if I raise up the hood and jiggle a few wires. See if that helps."

Anna pointed a shaking finger at the door. "You open that door, it's going to get even colder in here."

"I think it's worth the risk. If it produces heat, it'll be worth it."

Anna clung to her sleeve. "I don't want you to die out there."

Beth pushed her off. "I don't want you to die in here. I want to get you warmed up. This could work. I'm going to try it."

"You couldn't save Ellen so you want to save me?"

Beth blew out a breath. "Think of Jason. You can't have him coming home to an empty house tomorrow. We've got to get you warmed up."

Beth strained against the door, battling the wind, then squeezed her body out through the opening and slammed it behind her. Anna couldn't see her in the darkness outside the car, but she felt the hood rattle, heard it lift . . . she was shaking so badly now she couldn't hear anything unless she held her breath . . . she began to count in her head, giving Beth to the count of three-hundred—five minutes, she figured—to get back into the car. If she didn't get back by the count of three-hundred, Anna would have to go outside and drag her back in. Otherwise, Beth would freeze out there. Could a person freeze to death in this weather? It wasn't like the North Pole, she didn't think it was below zero; hypothermia was the thing that could kill you here, she guessed, but she didn't really know. Eric would know. Eric would figure out how to build a fire and keep them warm. There was enough gas in the car for fuel, but how to ignite it? If only one of them smoked.... Beth had said her mother smoked ... said she remembered the thick clouds of it in the house. Anna had tried to imagine it, growing up in a trailer as Beth had, so poor they didn't even have beds. One couch. Two mattresses. A crate for a table. The shotgun was the only thing handed down in her mother's family, the only thing left to her by her own father, the bastard, forcing Beth's mother out of the house when she was pregnant with Beth.

How was it that Beth's mother could even afford cigarettes?

Anna's arms felt heavy. Her head throbbed, but it was less painful now, numbing she guessed with the cold. She closed her eyes, listening to the ice still coming down hard on the roof of the car. It was difficult to care, but Beth cared; that was enough. That meant Anna could relax, let herself float....

Her mother would want her to set the table for dinner ... fork on the left, knife and spoon on the right, fold the napkins just so. Light the candles. Put ice in the glasses. Dinner on the verandah? Or was there a storm? Eric walked up the road, bending to kiss her. Two-hundred fifty-one. Two-hundred fifty-two. Why was she counting? Oh yes, Beth was out there jiggling the wires.

"Beth?" she called.

The car rattled and shook. Beth must be doing something out there, fixing up the engine. And she wasn't even a man! She loved Beth, loved her fiercely. Had loved her for years. Beth with her chain saw out in the country cutting up wood for her stove. Beth with her welding tools making her sculptures. Beth in her hard hat leading the way through a cave, Anna holding tight to her hand. "If anyone can get us out of here, you can," Anna had said.

Anna opened her door. "Beth!" The wind caught her name, hurled it across the mountain. "Beth!"

Another explosion. Tree limb? Whole tree? In the darkness, it was impossible to tell, and the wind cut through Anna's thin clothes. She could hardly control her legs to move her feet out the door, her sneakers disappearing into the snow. "Beth!"

A few strong men could easily lift this little car.

She felt her way around to the hood. "Beth!"

"What the fuck are you doing out here?" Beth spoke from beneath the hood of the car. "Get back in there and try the engine."

"Oh, God." Anna clung to her coat. "I thought you wanted to die. I thought you were dead."

"Get back in the fucking car!" Beth said.

Anna made her way to the open car door, commanded her legs to lift themselves in, turned the key and heard the chug-chug of a cold engine. Clicked it off and tried again. Chug-chug and then it caught, the car was running. Cold air blasted from the vents, but it would warm up soon, it would be all right. Beth was back in the car now, and she was saying something ... what? ... Anna wanted to sleep, to slide down on the seat and put her head in Beth's lap ... but Beth was pulling off Anna's wet clothes, pressing her body against Anna's ... Anna wanted to push her off, but she couldn't make herself speak or move ... Beth lay Anna down, Anna's front to the heater vents, Beth's front curled around Anna's back, and held her body against Anna's. She put her own hat on Anna's head and her socks on Anna's feet. She took off her jacket, her sweater, her pants, and wrapped the clothes around the two of them.

"Try to stay awake," Beth was saying. "I'm going to warm your body with my body. Your clothes are still soaking wet.

They're just making you colder."

Anna pressed her teeth together. Tasted blood. There was that fish that had been up on its tail. Saying what?

"Come on," Beth said. Anna's cold skin against her warm skin. Anna's hair in her mouth, Anna's back against Beth's flat belly. Now the air from the vents was warming. Heat from the vents roared, as it had roared from the vent just outside the closet where she'd hidden that day, covering her ears.

"Someone put a blanket over the body before you got home," the policeman had said to her mother. "Someone else found the body first. Was it the other little girl? Was it you, honey?" He looked at Beth.

Beth shook her head. "Not me, not me." She squeezed her eyes shut. She had not seen her sister playing with the gun. She had been watching some dumb show on TV—Gilligan's Island—and they were about to get off the island, there was an airplane, they would be saved; no more nights without the "Telly," as Mr. Howell called it, and "Lovey" could finally have a proper maid. The commercial for Rice Krispies came on and she looked at the dinette where the man was listening to his cereal. It was like the one she'd seen over at her friend Tammy's. One day she'd have one like that, too, and art on the walls like she'd seen in the picture books, maybe even marble sculptures. They'd live in a real house, one with a screened-in porch and a fenced yard, where they could keep a puppy. She had not said to Ellen, No, you don't play with that, because she had been in this other world, not in the trailer with the plastic-covered windows where her mother kept a loaded shotgun in the closet because, as she said, you never know out here in the country. They said Ellen must have been looking into the barrel when the gun went off, must have been wondering what was in there. She wore her red corduroy coveralls. Beth touched her bare feet, her chubby toes. Ellen's feet looked cold. She put a blanket over her sister's feet.

The rest of her sister was covered in blood, so Beth hadn't been able to hold her like this, hadn't been able to warm her sister, and now she could. She held Ellen tight. She wrapped her arms around her sister.

Anna stirred. "Sweetie," she said to Eric. "I went up the mountain." She snuggled deeper into Beth's arms. "Did you pick up the milk?"

Even when the fuel tank emptied, they kept each other warm, hearts pumping the blood through the cells of their skin until the ice storm let up, until they rubbed the fog of their breaths from the windshield and, in the morning, looked out on a world of snapped trees and fallen branches, shards of tree trunks glittering.

ACKNOWLEDGMENTS

Thanks to Al Young, the contest judge who chose this book, and to Patty Seyburn and Gloria Vando Hickok, who—with Helicon Nine—effected the miracle of a first book publication. The stories were written over a period of 12 years, so there are many people who mattered along the way.

The encouragement of friends from writing groups in Oregon, Idaho, and Virginia, has been invaluable, particularly Kim Barnes, Barbara Carlisle, Audrey Colombe, Collin Hughes, LuAnn Keener, Buddy Levy, Simone Poirier-Bures, Bonnie Soniat, Anita Sullivan, Dave Toomey, Jane Varley, and Gyorgyi Voros. Thanks also to Fishtrap, Inc., for providing a Western home and to Pam Steele and Jan Alden for making it all the more hospitable. Steve and Clo Gibson cheered early drafts of these stories. Betty Campbell and Ted Leeson, were essential friends. Linda Tross not only provided a beautiful cover but also enduring friendship. Jenny Zia coached and listened. Carol Bailey gave me the courage to color outside the lines.

Many teachers offered generous support within and beyond the classroom, especially Sharon Haring; also Janne Goldbeck, Richard McCann, Kermit Moyer, Kim Stafford, Henry Taylor, and Jean Valentine.

Jody and Tom Southall and Kiel Norris, as well as their children; also Margie Laquatra, and the extended Norris family, offered unfailing support as well as an invaluable sense of belonging.

My parents, Carrie and Wayne Norris, have quite simply been essential. They've provided help of all kinds before I could even think to ask.

Without Ed Falco's encouragement and example as a writer, this book would not exist. Susan Falco and Will Stauffer-Norris surprise, humble, teach and delight me day by day.

Biographical Note

Lisa Norris has seen life from several parts of the country and world. Growing up as part of a Navy family, she lived in several states and the Philippines. After she earned a forestry degree from Virginia Tech and worked as a fire dispatcher, trail ranger, and biological technician, she moved to Idaho and earned an M.A. in English from Idaho State University. She taught English and creative writing in Idaho and Oregon for ten years, then moved to Washington, D.C., where she completed her M.F.A. in creative writing from American University. She now teaches in the English Department at Virginia Tech and lives in Blacksburg, Virginia, with her family. Her work has been published in a variety of literary magazines. *Toy Guns* is her first book.

OTHER BOOKS BY HELICON NINE EDITIONS

FICTION

One Girl, a novel in stories by Sheila Kohler. Winner of the
1998 Willa Cather Fiction Prize. Selected by William Gass.

Climbing the God Tree, a novel in stories by Jaimee Wriston Colbert.
1997 Willa Cather Fiction Prizewinner. Selected by Dawn Raffel.

Eternal City, a first collection of stories by Molly Shapiro. Winner of the
1996 Willa Cather Fiction Prize. Selected by Hilary Masters.

Knucklebones, 27 short stories by Annabel Thomas.
1994 Willa Cather Fiction Prizewinner. Selected by Daniel Stern.

Galaxy Girls:Wonder Women, stories by Anne Whitney Pierce.
1993 Willa Cather Fiction Prizewinner. Selected by Carolyn Doty.

Return to Sender, a first novel by Ann Slegman.

The Value of Kindness, short stories by Ellyn Bache,
1992 Willa Cather Fiction Prizewinner. Selected by James Byron Hall.

Italian Smoking Piece with Simultaneous Translation, by Christy Sheffield-Sanford.
A multi-dimensional tour de force.

Sweet Angel Band, a first book of stories by Rose Marie Kinder.
1991 Willa Cather Fiction Prizewinner. Selected by Robley Wilson.

POETRY

The Air Lost in Breathing, a first book of poems by Simone Muench. Winner of the
1999 Marianne Moore Poetry Prize. Selected by Charlie Smith.

Flesh, a first book of poems by Susan Gubernat. Winner of the
1998 Marianne Moore Poetry Prize. Selected by Robert Phillips.

Diasporadic, a first book of poems by Patty Seyburn. Winner of the
1997 Marianne Moore Poetry Prize. Selected by Molly Peacock. Received the
2000 Notable Book Award for Poetry (American Library Association).

On Days Like This, poems about baseball and life by the late Dan Quisenberry.,
one of America's favorite pitchers.

Prayers to the Other Life, a first book of poems by Christopher Seid. Winner of the
1996 Marianne Moore Poetry Prize. Selected by David Ray.

A Strange Heart, a second book of poems by Jane O. Wayne. Winner of the
1995 Marianne Moore Poetry Prize. Selected by James Tate. Received the
1996 Society of Midland Authors Poetry Competition Award.

Without Warning, a second book of poems by Elizabeth Goldring.
Co-published with BkMk Press, University of Missouri-Kansas City.

Night Drawings, a first book of poems by Marjorie Stelmach. Winner of the
1994 Marianne Moore Poetry Prize. Introduction by David Ignatow, judge.

Wool Highways, poems of New Zealand by David Ray. Winner of the 1993 William Carlos Williams Poetry Award (Poetry Society of America).

My Journey Toward You, a first book of poems by Judy Longley. Winner of the 1993 Marianne Moore Poetry Prize. Introduction by Richard Howard, judge.

Women in Cars, a first book of poems by Martha McFerren. Winner of the 1992 Marianne Moore Poetry Prize. Introduction by Colette Inez, judge.

Hoofbeats on the Door, a first book of poems by Regina deCormier. Introduction by Richard Howard.

Black Method, a first book of poems by Biff Russ. Winner of the 1991 Marianne Moore Poetry Prize. Introduction by Mona Van Duyn, judge.

ANTHOLOGIES

Spud Songs: An Anthology of Potato Poems, edited by Gloria Vando and Robert Stewart. Proceeds to benefit Hunger Relief.

Poets at Large: 25 Poets in 25 Homes, edited by H.L. Hix. A gathering of 25 poets in Kansas City commemorating National Poetry Month.

The Helicon Nine Reader: A Celebration of Women in the Arts., edited by Gloria Vando Hickok. The best of ten years of *Helicon Nine: The Journal of Women's Arts & Letters*.

FEUILLETS

Limited editions of little books, ranging in length from 4–24 pages, accompanied by a mailing envelope.

Ancient Musics, a poetry sequence by Albert Goldbarth.

A Walk through the Human Heart, a poem by Robley Wilson.

Christmas 1956, a poem by Keith Denniston.

Climatron, a poem by Robert Stewart.

Cortége, a poem by Carl Phillips.

Down & In, poems by Dan Quisenberry.

Dresden, a poem by Patricia Cleary Miller.

Generations, a poem by George Wedge.

The Heart, a short story by Catherine Browder.

R. I. P., a poem by E.S. Miller.

Short Prose, an illustrated essay by M. Kasper.

Slivers, a poem by Philip Miller.

Stravinsky's Dream, a story by Conger Beasley, Jr.

This is how they were placed for us, a poem by Luci Tapahonso.

Tokens, a poem by Judy Ray.